D0402686

THE MUSIC OF ZOMBIES

TALES FROM THE FIVE KINGDOMS:

The Robe of Skulls

The Bag of Bones

The Heart of Glass

The Flight of Dragons

The Fifth Tale from
THE FIVE KINGDOMS

THE
MUSIC OF ZOMBIES

VIVIAN FRENCH

ILLUSTRATED BY ROSS COLLINS

CANDLEWICK PRESS

Text copyright © 2012 by Vivian French
Illustrations copyright © 2012 by Ross Collins

First U.S. edition 2013

Library of Congress Catalog Card Number 2012943656
ISBN 978-0-7636-5930-1

13 14 15 16 17 18 BVG 10 9 8 7 6 5 4 3 2 1

Printed in Berryville, VA, U.S.A.

This book was typeset in Baskerville.

Candlewick Press
99 Dover Street
Somerville, Massachusetts 02144

visit us at www.candlewick.com

For Genevieve Herr,
with much love and admiration

xxx

PRINCIPAL CHARACTERS

Prince Marcus	second in line to the throne of Gorebreath
Gracie Gillypot	a Trueheart
Gubble	a domesticated troll
Marlon	a bat
Alf	Marlon's nephew
Auntie Vera	Marlon's auntie
Prince Albion	Prince of Cockenzie Rood
Prince Arioso	Marcus's twin brother, first in line to the throne of Gorebreath
Hortense	Albion's cousin, Dowager Duchess of Cockenzie Rood
Queen Bluebell	Queen of Wadingburn
King Frank	King of Gorebreath
Queen Mildred	Queen of Gorebreath
Queen Kesta	Queen of Dreghorn
Princess Nina-Rose	Princess of Dreghorn
Fiddleduster Squint	a zombie
Shadow	a shadow
Gruntle Marrowgrease	landlord of the Howling Arms
Marley Bagsmith	royal spy appointed by Prince Albion

THE GIANTS
Greatover • Meggymould • Trunkly

THE ANCIENT CRONES

Edna	the Ancient One
Elsie	the Oldest
Val	the Youngest
Foyce	Gracie's stepsister and apprentice crone

Chapter One

Prince Marcus was asleep. From the other side of the council chamber, his father glared at him; Marcus remained oblivious. His twin, Prince Arioso, older by ten minutes and heir to the throne of Gorebreath, was making his first official speech. Marcus's eyelids had drooped after the first twenty minutes, and by the end of an hour, he had given up all attempts to stay awake. Fortunately, Arioso was blissfully unaware of his brother's sleeping form draped over a couple of chairs.

"And I do think," Arry went on, "that we in Gorebreath are particularly blessed that our subjects are, without a doubt, the most hardworking, loyal, and respectable in all of the Five Kingdoms."

The variously assorted guests nodded their appreciation and looked pleased with themselves. Marley

Bagsmith, who came from Cockenzie Rood and had sneaked in without an invitation, looked sour.

Arioso beamed at his audience. "You can always be relied upon to be loyal, and I know you are respectable and hardworking under all circumstances, and I am truly honored to be your prince. Today, as you well know, is Gorebreath Day, the day when we come together to celebrate our wonderful kingdom and our respectable, hardworking, and loyal subjects, and I am truly honored and ever so delighted to have this opportunity to thank those of you who are here in person for all your hard work and loyalty and respectability, and to end by saying—"

Arioso's final words were lost. Marcus, dreaming of adventures far outside the borders of the Five Kingdoms, twitched, yelped, and fell off his chair. The guests stared, openmouthed. Arry was shocked into silence. As King Frank rose from his throne, his face purple with anger, Marcus scrambled to his feet. He took one look at his father, muttered an indistinct apology, and made a dash for the door, slamming it behind him. A small bat who had been dozing on top of a statue in the corridor woke with a start as Marcus hurtled past.

"Yikes!" he remarked. "What happened there? Pants on fire?" And he flew after the hurrying prince.

Back in the council chamber, King Frank took a deep breath and held up his hand to quell the speculative murmurs and whispers. "Ladies and gentlemen, please forgive my younger son. He . . . he has . . . he has not been well. Flu. Erm. Yes. Flu. So please excuse him. But in the meantime, I'm sure you'll wish to join me in thanking Prince Arioso and agree with me that he will be a worthy king of Gorebreath one day."

"Which we hope won't be for a long, long time, Father." Arry had recovered, and the palace guests applauded enthusiastically, hoping that this meant the speeches were finally over and they could head for the royal dining room. Gorebreath Day was traditionally celebrated with excessive quantities of food and drink, and the palace cook had a splendid reputation.

"Indeed. Thank you, dear boy. Thank you so much." King Frank clapped Arioso on the back. "I have to say that I join you in that hope. But before we end today's celebrations, I would like to say a few words myself."

The guests sank back in their seats. Slumped in the back row, Farmer Netherwood elbowed his daughter. "Where's that Bagsmith fella gone? Skipped, by the look of things. Must have slithered like an eel to get out without me noticing. Right here beside me, he was."

"Hush, Dad." Susie Netherwood took royal occasions seriously. "Never you mind what them furriners get up to. Be quiet now, and listen to His Majesty."

Farmer Netherwood did as he was told with a reluctant grunt. King Frank had produced a sizable handful of notes from his pocket and had already launched into a detailed account of the recent scumball match between Gorebreath and Niven's Knowe. As he described each and every move with comments, criticisms, and an excessive waving of his arms, even Prince Arioso's smile began to fade. Queen Mildred sighed. She was worried about Marcus, but there was no chance of finding out what he was up to until his father had finished talking. She sighed again and wished she had asked for an extra cushion.

Outside the palace, Marcus was heading for the stables at a run.

Chapter Two

Marley Bagsmith was not a pleasant man. He was small and wizened, and as cunning as a weasel. He had a quick brain but, up until the morning of Gorebreath Day, had never found a position that he felt suited his personality . . . a position that paid well, required little action, and allowed him to spend a good deal of time in an extremely dubious inn called the Howling Arms. Now, however, he believed he had found the perfect occupation. Marley Bagsmith had, as of that very morning, been appointed Royal Spy.

His previous position as third washer of dishes in the Royal Palace of Cockenzie Rood had proved less than satisfactory. The work was hard, the hours long, and the pay minimal. After three days Marley had decided that enough was enough and had walked away from the kitchens with a spring in his step. He did not, however, walk away from the palace. He had been working in the kitchens long enough to notice the splendid fruit and vegetables that were always available, and he had a plan. Swinging around the corner of the huge stone walls, he headed for the royal vegetable gardens; even though it was early, there was already a young gardener carrying a basket and picking handfuls of fresh peas. Marley grinned and fingered the heavy iron ladle he had awarded himself as a going-away present.

Five minutes later it was Marley, now swathed in the official apron of the Cockenzie Rood Royal Gardeners' Association, who was picking peas. And carrots. And onions. And cauliflowers. And cabbages. He took no notice of the faint groans issuing from a nearby shed and continued to fill the basket while calculating how much he could get for the contents from the local street market. As the total rose, Marley's whistle grew cheerier, and, when the basket could take no more, he set off at a brisk trot for the back gate. On the way he passed a kitchen maid with an armful of flowers, but she gave no sign of recognizing him.

"You're a smart guy," Marley told himself. "Look as if you know what you're doing, and no one'll challenge you!" He glanced back as the girl hurried away, then turned—to find himself walking straight into the substantial form of Prince Albion. Vegetables tumbled in all directions as the prince doubled over, clutching his stomach.

"Urf," he said. "Urf."

Marley's mind had never worked so fast. He leaped into the air with a loud yell, hurling the basket into the distance. "Look out, Your Highness! There may be more of them!"

"What, what, what, what?" Prince Albion went pale. "What? What is it? Where? What's happening?"

Marley Bagsmith stared over the prince's shoulder with an expression of extreme ferocity. "Whoever you are," he shouted, "I'm here to protect our noble prince! Do your worst—you'll have to deal with me!" Shaking his fist for additional effect, he squinted sideways to make sure Albion was watching.

"Did . . . did someone just try to attack me?" The prince's voice was trembling.

Marley squared his shoulders. "Indeed, they did, Your Highness. Good thing I was here. My goodness me, yes. Why, those carrots could have done you a lot of damage if I hadn't thrown myself in the way."

"Carrots? Oh, dearie, dearie me. Look at them all! And cabbages too! How . . . how terrible to

be attacked by a cabbage!" Albion peered around nervously. "Do you think they'll try again?"

"No, Your Highness." Marley squinted into the distance. "I'd say I scared them off good and proper."

The prince sat down suddenly in the middle of the path. Pulling out his handkerchief, he began to wipe his face. "Who can it have been? Oh, my goodness. What a shock! You saved me, you know. I should give you a reward. I'm sure I should."

Marley Bagsmith's smile stretched from ear to ear, giving him the look of a lean and hungry wolf.

The prince hastily put away his handkerchief and struggled to his feet. "Actually, now that I come to think about it, maybe I should ask Pa. Or Cousin Hortense. She gets ever so cross if I give rewards without asking."

Marley's smile dimmed. King Dowby spent his days in the royal stables or riding over the hills and had no interest in anything that did not have four legs, a mane, and a tail, but Hortense, the dowager duchess, was not a woman who could be easily fooled. "No, no, Your Highness." He shook his head. "I wouldn't dream of taking a reward for doing my duty. But a job, perhaps . . . that would be a great kindness." He gave the prince a sly wink. "And you'd not need to ask your cousin about that, would you?"

Albion looked blank. "Aren't you a gardener?"

"A gardener? What . . . oh, no." Marley dropped the gardener's apron onto the path and pushed it away with his foot. An idea floated into his devious and self-serving mind, and he clasped his hands to his chest in a sudden, dramatic gesture. "I was wearing that as a disguise, Your Highness. A disguise, so nobody would suspect I was here to guard my prince from danger."

The heir to the throne of Cockenzie Rood was not clever. Adding five and eleven was a major challenge, and multiplication sums gave him a rash. All the same, he was beginning to suspect that all was not exactly as it had first appeared. He frowned. "But if you're not a gardener, why were you in my garden?"

Marley put his finger to his nose and winked again. "Heard a rumor, Your Highness. When I was in Gorebreath . . ." For a moment his imagination failed him, and he hesitated. He had, however, unwittingly struck a chord.

Prince Albion's eyes narrowed. "Gorebreath? Gorebreath, did you say? Now, that doesn't surprise me. There's always been trouble there. I blame Marcus, you know. Arioso's a splendid chap, simply splendid, but Marcus never has behaved himself properly, and it gives people ideas. Never a good thing. My dear old grandpa used to say that ideas were worse than gunpowder for causing trouble."

"Exactly, Your Highness." Marley nodded enthusiastically. "Just so. That's why I thought I'd have a look around."

"So were you spying? Are you a spy?" Albion's watery blue eyes shone.

"Hush—if you'll excuse me saying so, Your Highness." Marley's voice was a confidential whisper. "Let's keep that word as our little secret."

The prince blinked. "A spy. Oh, my goodness. How just too terribly thrilling! Did Cousin Hortense ask you here? Did she want you to look after me?"

Marley tapped his nose for the second time. "Not the duchess, Your Highness. It was"—he paused to cough modestly—"my own idea. I'm of the opinion, if you'll excuse a poor man but one of your most loyal subjects, that we need to be very careful these days. Whispers, rumors . . . one kingdom setting itself against another. Gorebreath, Niven's Knowe, Dreghorn, Wadingburn . . . all of them are sure to be jealous of Cockenzie Rood, and who can blame them, says I? So I thought to myself, what does our noble Prince Albion need to keep him safe? A spy. So, seeing as today is Gorebreath Day, and the inhabitants of Gorebreath are likely to be overexcited and up to all sorts of things, I came to this here vegetable garden this morning—and what did I find? Trouble. Bad trouble." Marley shook his head mournfully. "But if I was acting out of turn, Your Highness, you just say the word, and I'll make myself scarce."

"A spy. My very own spy." The prince considered the suggestion. "Hmm . . . I like it! It's a super idea! So you'll be watching out for me . . . just me? Not Pa? Or Cousin Hortense?"

Marley bowed. "Just you, Your Highness."

"Super!" Albion gave a bounce of excitement. "Super-duper! Can you start at once?"

Marley bowed again, and Albion beamed at him. "What can you do first? I know! You can go to Gorebreath and see what they're saying. See if they talk about me! They have speeches on Gorebreath Day, you know. Lots of speeches! Oh, and you can see what else they are up to. We've got Cockenzie Rood Day next Thursday, and Cousin Hortense'll be away in Wadingburn. She's ever so cross about it because it means Pa's officially in charge, and he never remembers to do anything she tells him. She's written everything down, and I'm to check that it gets done properly." A shifty expression floated across the prince's large pasty face. "Don't tell, but I'm thinking of changing things. Just a teensy little bit, so everyone knows how special I am, and how I can make decisions all by my very own self. Pa won't mind. He'll never know, actually. He'll be off on a horse somewhere." Albion waved a pudgy hand to dismiss his father. "I've got some super-duper ideas. Trumpets, marching, singing, talent competition—that sort of thing. Been looking in the history books, you know, and they did things differently in the old days. Much more fun! Songs in honor of the prince, and dances in honor of the prince, and competitions for the prince to judge, and all sorts of things! But you can see what goes on at Gorebreath and tell me all about it. Come here tomorrow morning, here in the gardens. Super-duper! Oh! I nearly forgot. What's your name?"

Given his new status as a spy, Marley decided the truth would be best avoided. "Bill Barley, Your Highness. And honored to work for such a noble as you. Erm . . . might I ask what the financial situation might be?"

His new employer thrust a hand into his pockets and brought out a collection of loose change. Seeing gold among the silver, Marley's eyes gleamed. "That'll do nicely for the time being," he said as casually as he could. "Expenses extra, of course, but Your Highness will be expecting that."

Prince Albion nodded. "Expenses extra. Of course. Super. Now, run along, Bill Barley—WHAT'S THAT?"

The prince had heard a moan. A loud moan, followed by another, and then another.

Marley cursed under his breath. Would the under-gardener point him out as his attacker? Darting to the shed, he pulled the door open and the boy staggered out.

"Hit me over the head, they did! Hit me over the head!"

Prince Albion gave a shrill scream. "Help! Call the guard! We've been invaded! Help! Help!" And he set off toward the palace as fast as his portly legs would carry him.

The under-gardener propped himself against the shed wall but gave no sign of recognizing Marley. "Did you see them, sir, did you see them? Loads of them, there was, all armed to the teeth!"

Marley heaved a sigh of relief. "Terrible times we live in," he agreed. "Terrible. You'd best get down to the kitchen and get that bump seen to. I've got a job to do. Private business for His Highness. Ta-ta for now!" And jangling the coins in his pocket, he slid through a gap in the hedge and set off for Gorebreath.

Chapter Three

Far away from the Five Kingdoms, in the House of the Ancient Crones, Gracie Gillypot was untangling a tangled skein of scarlet wool. Behind her two looms were steadily clicking and clacking; on one lay a half-finished length of scarlet cloth, on the other the web of power shone with a smooth silver gleam.

"No trouble showing on the web," said the Oldest, as she threw the shuttle steadily to and fro. "Just like silk."

"Be quiet, Elsie." The Youngest frowned. "Don't tempt fate. The last thing I want to do just now is worry about the Five Kingdoms. If the web is looking nice and peaceful, be grateful for small mercies, is what I say. We've got another five cloaks to make before Cockenzie Rood Day, and I don't see how we're going to get them done."

"Don't go expecting me to do any overtime," said a grumpy voice from a shadowed corner of the room. "I'm worn out already. And Gracie's late getting our tea. Again."

Gracie put down the wool and stood up. "Sorry, Foyce. I'll go and put the kettle on."

"Humph." Foyce settled herself back in her armchair and closed her eyes. "Lazy little worm."

Elsie tut-tutted disapprovingly. "Now, now, Foyce. That's no way to speak about your sister."

"*Step*sister," Foyce growled. "My dad made the biggest mistake of his life when he married her mom. She had the sense to lie down and die, but the nasty little worm came along as part of the deal, and we were stuck with her. No relation of mine would ever be such a mimsy-wimsy namby-pamby—"

"That's enough." The Youngest was sitting up very straight, her eyes flashing. "Gracie's a Trueheart, and what's more she's our much-loved adopted niece, so we'll have no more of your sour remarks, Miss Foyce Undershaft. You're here for a reason, in case you've forgotten—you're here to put your wicked ways behind you and learn how to be good. That's what Elsie and I had to do, and if we managed it, then you can too!"

"Okey-dokey. Don't get your knickers in a twist." Foyce yawned. "I need my tea."

"I'm on my way right now," Gracie told her, but at that moment the door opened and the Ancient One came in carrying a tray piled high with hot buttered toast. A large teapot was balanced precariously on the top of a pile of plates. Behind her stumped a squat green figure carrying a milk jug.

"Ug," it said as it put the jug down. "Ug."

"Thank you, Gubble." The Ancient One patted the troll's head. "Gracie dear, I'm so sorry—I've forgotten to bring the sugar, and I know Gubble can't drink tea without at least six spoonfuls. Could you fetch it?"

Gracie nodded. "Of course, Auntie Edna. Come on, Gubble. You can go with me."

"Ug." Gubble gave the toast a wistful glance, but turned and obediently followed Gracie out.

All the doors were amusing themselves by sliding up and down the long narrow corridor, and it took Gracie several moments to find WATER WINGS. "Sometimes I wish we lived in a house where things stayed put," she said as she caught at the door handle. "This house is lovely, and I wouldn't ever want to live anywhere else, but when you're in a hurry, it can be very inconvenient. I suppose it's something to do with living on the edge of the Wild Enchanted Forest. And whoever thought of calling a kitchen 'WATER WINGS'? No wonder Marcus gets muddled every time he comes here."

"Prince come today?" Gubble asked hopefully.

"Not today." Gracie suppressed a sigh. "It's Gorebreath Day, and he's got to be at the palace, listening to speeches. And then they have a feast, and he has to go around being polite to everyone. It sounds dreadful." She rattled the handle. "Why won't this door open?"

Gubble grunted. "Bad door," he said, and kicked it.

"Oh, GUBBLE!" Gracie gazed in horror at the splintered hole. The door drooped on its hinges, and Gracie gave it an apologetic pat as she went through into the kitchen. "Gubble, I don't think you deserve any tea, I really don't."

The troll, unrepentant, advanced toward the table and began to help himself to spoonfuls of sugar. Gracie leaned across, removed the bowl, and shut it in a cupboard. "No," she said firmly. "And now you can help me sweep up the mess you've made."

Gubble looked up at her. "Gracie cross with Gubble?"

"I am a bit," Gracie admitted. "Now, where's the dustpan and brush?" She went to look in a cupboard, but before she could open it, there was a loud knock at the back door.

"Bother," she said. "Who can that be? We aren't expecting anyone, are we?"

The troll shook his head. "Ug."

Gracie frowned. "I do hope it's not another order for cloaks. Auntie Edna and Auntie Elsie have been working nonstop for days, and Auntie Val's doing overtime, and Foyce is about to go on strike." She smiled at Gubble. "Maybe we'll have to train you to do some weaving."

Gubble looked horrified, and Gracie laughed as she went to open the door. It was in its right and proper place but had turned itself upside down, and Gracie wasn't tall enough to reach the bolt. She was about to fetch a chair to stand on when the mail slot rattled and a voice called, "Gracie! Gracie—it's me!"

The door immediately swiveled around and opened itself in welcome, revealing a hot and dusty prince on the doorstep. "Hi," Marcus said as he stepped inside. "I'm really sorry to barge in without letting you know I was coming, but I've had the most dreadful day and I don't think Father will ever speak to me again, and the only person I really wanted to see was you."

"Oh!" Gracie, to her intense mortification, found herself blushing. "That's . . . I mean, thank you. Come in!"

"Cuppa tea," said a voice from the corridor. "Prince need cuppa tea."

Gracie gave Gubble a grateful glance. "Of course — would you like some tea?"

Marcus grinned. "I don't suppose there's any chance of something to eat, is there? I'm starving!"

"I could make you some scrambled eggs, if you'd like." Hoping that the lights were dim enough to hide her glowing cheeks, Gracie led the way back to WATER WINGS.

Marcus looked at the damaged door with interest. "What happened here?"

"Gubble was in a hurry," Gracie explained. "I don't know what the crones are going to say. We were just about to sweep the mess up when you arrived. I can do it later, though. How many eggs would you like? We've got loads — Auntie Elsie's taken to keeping hens. Oh — and why won't your father speak to you?"

"Mr. Prince is on the run. Came out of the throne room like, if you'll excuse the expression, Miss Gracie, a bat out of hell!"

The voice was small and squeaky, and Gracie smiled as she looked up into the corner.

"Hello, Alf! When did you get here?"

"Followed Mr. Prince," the little bat said cheerfully. "Knew there was something up. Is it an adventure?"

Marcus sat down, groaned, and put his head on the table. "No. I wish it was. I . . . I went to sleep during Arry's speech, and I fell off my chair. That woke me up, of course, and all I could think was to get out of there as fast as I could. Father looked FURIOUS! Oh, what am I going to do?"

Gracie looked down at the despondent figure. Should she give him a hug? The thought made her heart beat faster. A consoling pat might be more suitable, she decided, but a series of squeaks made her glance up at the curtain rail instead.

"Oh, Mr. Prince! You are the best!" Alf waved a wing while he tried to control his laughter. "Ma says the only way she could ever get me to sleep when I was a baby was by reciting one of King Frank's speeches . . . and now — *hic-hic-hic!* — Prince Arry's doing it too! Only he's sending his brother to sleep! Oh, *hic-hic-hic-HIC!*"

Marcus sat up. For a moment Gracie wondered if he was offended, but a huge smile gradually spread across his face, and a moment later they were all laughing while Marcus, in between gasps for breath, recited "loyal, respectable, and hardworking" over and over again.

Chapter Four

Prince Albion had spent the day in a flutter of anxiety. The Dowager Duchess of Cockenzie Rood had dismissed his story of invaders with a flick of her wrist and a resolute refusal to call out the army. "Nonsense, Albion," she had said. "Why on earth would anyone start an invasion in the vegetable garden?"

Even after the under-gardener had been produced, and the bump on his head demonstrated as evidence of a ferocious and armed enemy presence, Hortense had remained unimpressed. "Did you *see* anyone hit you, Lubbidge?" she asked.

Lubbidge confessed that he hadn't.

"And did you see any strangers in the garden before you were hit on the head?"

Lubbidge, after some long thought, had to admit that he had seen nobody.

"Thank you, Lubbidge." The duchess waved the under-gardener away. "There, Albion. Not the slightest sign of an invader."

"But he was shut in the shed, cuz," Albion argued. "He couldn't possibly have shut himself in. Bill—I mean, someone who was there in the garden with me—had to let him out."

The duchess gave the prince a sharp look. "Bill?"

Albion stood on one leg and coughed. "A . . . that is . . . someone who works for me."

Hortense's eyebrows rose. "Indeed?"

"Yes. It was someone who . . . who is sort of looking after me. I suppose I am allowed to have someone if I want? Someone who cares about me and is there to save me from mad carrot throwers and boppings on the head!" Albion's voice was growing shrill, and the duchess's suspicions were confirmed.

"You're up to something, Albion," she announced. "I suppose you've persuaded some unfortunate peasant to be your bodyguard. Hmm. Well, I suppose it can't do any harm, just as long as you promise me you won't pay him vast sums of money. I know you all too well. No idea of what things cost."

The prince scowled. He and his cousin had a fractious relationship. She had arrived to look after

him when his mother died and was as different from Queen Malliena as chalk from cheese. The queen had indulged Albion in every way; the duchess believed in cold showers, brisk walks, cake only after you had eaten your bread and butter, and—first and fore-most—Duty to the Kingdom. She was, however, fond of her young cousin and did her best to set him along the right path without being too strict.

"You see," she had once explained to her very good friend Queen Bluebell of Wadingburn, "Albion never had much of a chance. Look at his father! Never sets foot in the palace. You'd need to put hooves on the boy before his father would take any notice of him."

"Doesn't Albion ride, then?" Queen Bluebell had asked.

"Albion? Never. He was shown a horse when he was six months old, and he screamed himself purple. Ever since then Dowby's ignored him."

"Humph." Bluebell had considered the situation. "Dowby never did have any sense. Used to catch wasps when he was a boy, then wonder why they stung him. No idea what those horses see in him. But I suppose he is Albion's father. Oh, well. At least Albion's got you, Hortense, and you're a sensible gal."

✴ ✴ ✴

Albion, quite unaware of the sensible gal's affection and genuine concern for his welfare, went on scowling. "I was attacked. Someone tried to hit me with a carrot. I need to be protected!"

Hortense sighed. "Of course you do, Albion dear. And if anything like this happens again, I'll make sure there's a full investigation. Now, why don't we run through the list of events on Cockenzie Rood Day? After all—" The duchess paused. Was it hypocritical to use a little flattery? Probably not. She went on, "After all, your father's very unlikely to stay after he's made his introductory speech, so you'll be left in charge, and I'm sure you'll manage extremely well."

The prince brightened. "I will, won't I?" The flattery soothed his irritation, and he beamed at his cousin. "I'll be Top Royal! Ha! It'll be the best Cockenzie Rood Day ever! Come on, cuz. Let's go and look at the plans." He gave a little skip. "I can't WAIT until Thursday!"

"I'm so sorry I can't be there with you." This was not entirely true; the duchess was very much looking forward to spending time with her old friend Bluebell and avoiding a long day of speeches and general boredom, but it seemed unnecessary to say so. "Such a shame that your father chose the same day as Bluebell's birthday. It's never been a clash before."

Albion was suddenly transfixed by a bird flying overhead. He gazed at it with extreme interest while he tried to think of a way to avoid confessing that it was he who had chosen the date. His father, when presented with the 18th of the month instead of the traditional 21st, had made no objection; he had merely remarked that if the date didn't clash with the weekly visit of the farrier, Albion could do what he wanted when he wanted and where he wanted, just as long as he, King Dowby, was not required to do anything. Anything at all.

"Ah," Albion said at last. "Quite so . . . yes. Bad timing."

Hortense gave her young cousin a sideways look. "Are you quite sure you aren't worried about it?"

"Worried? Me? Oh, NO, Cousin Hortense. Why would I be worried? It'll be super-duper tip-top dandy, just you wait and see. Well, you won't see, will you, because you won't be there, but I'm sure everyone will tell you." Albion gave an emphatic nod. "Yes. Super-duper."

The duchess was now certain that Albion was hiding something, but she made the mistake of believing it was his desire to be allowed out in the public eye on his own. Had she known of his plans for a grand parade (led by Albion in full military uniform), a choral presentation (conducted by Albion in top hat and tails), a talent competition (to be judged by Albion, but also featuring Albion's rendition of the National Anthem), and a theatrical grand finale (starring Albion in the role of hero), she would have canceled her visit there and then.

"Well, well," she said kindly. "You must send a messenger as soon as it's over with a full report. I'll be longing to hear all the news!"

Chapter Five

Marcus—after a hearty meal of scrambled eggs, toast, cake, three apples, and a banana—was feeling much better. "Father can't exactly ground me," he told Gracie as they washed the dishes together. "I'm too old for that. I expect I'll just get a long and boring lecture, and then it'll all blow over. I'll have to tell him I'm incredibly sorry about it all, of course."

"Of course," Gracie agreed. "Will your brother be angry with you?"

"Arry?" Marcus grinned. "No. He'll see it as an excuse to Do a Noble Deed. He'll forgive me with a gracious smile, while secretly being thrilled to bits that I've given him yet another opportunity to show what an utterly splendid chap he is."

Gracie giggled. "He's not much like you, is he?"

Marcus shook his head. "No. Don't know where I came from. I think my entire family is pompous and boring, and they think I'm weird. They get palpitations at the very thought of an adventure." He stopped drying the teapot and gave Gracie a hopeful look. "I don't suppose there's anything brewing, is there? Like the web looking spotty? 'Cause that's what it does when there's evil sneaking about, doesn't it?"

"Auntie Val says that even if the web turns black, they won't have time to worry about it," Gracie told him. "They've got a huge order for Cockenzie Rood Day. Apparently Prince Albion's ordered a whole load of scarlet cloaks for a grand parade."

"Albion? What's he up to?" Marcus went back to polishing the teapot. "They never have parades on Cockenzie Rood Day."

"Well, they are this time." Edna was standing in the doorway with the tray of dirty tea things. "Nice to see you, Marcus! I wondered why Gracie hadn't come back with the sugar." She put the tray down on the table and gave the prince a considering look. "Am I right in thinking this is an unexpected visit?"

Marcus flushed. "Erm . . . yes. I . . . sort of left Gorebreath in a bit of a hurry. I'm going to have to do a lot of apologizing when I get back."

The Ancient One said nothing, but the look in her one bright blue eye made Marcus feel the need to explain further. "I fell asleep in the middle of Arioso's speech, and then I fell off my chair. It made a terrible ruckus, so I made a run for it."

Alf, who had been dozing on the curtain rail, woke up. "Ran to see his own true love," he said in sentimental tones, then sniggered. "Oooh! Miss Gracie! I've thought of a joke. You could say Mr. Prince ran to meet his own Trueheart love, couldn't you?"

Gracie, in an agony of embarrassment, frowned at him, but he took no notice. "Or you could say—"

The Ancient One snapped her fingers, and Alf was silenced. "So you ran here?" Marcus nodded. "Hmm. After falling asleep in the middle of your brother's first speech. I can quite see the need for an apology. And I'd suggest the sooner you get it over with the better." She glanced out of the window. "It's still light. If you leave now, you could be back before your parents decide you've run away and call out the army."

Marcus's eyes widened. "But—" he began.

Edna sniffed. "Silly boy. I wasn't suggesting you ride your pony. You wouldn't be back until the wee small hours of the morning. Seeing as it's something of an emergency, I'll send you home on the path. You can leave Glee here. Gracie'll look after him, and you can come and collect him whenever you like, just as long" — the one blue eye grew frosty — "just as long as you tell your parents where you're going."

"Oh, I will. Thank you very much, indeed." Marcus was genuinely grateful, and Edna smiled.

"Run along, then. Gracie, the path takes far more notice of you than me. See what you can do with it, and then come and help me with the dishes."

Gracie gave her adopted aunt a quick hug before leading Marcus outside. Alf flew above them, twittering happily, and Gubble stomped after Gracie. The path was frisking merrily up and down outside the house, but when Gracie whistled, it straightened itself and waited for instructions.

"Now, Path — listen carefully," she said. "Could you please take Prince Marcus back to Gorebreath? Quick as you can!" She gave it a small stroke, and the path wriggled with pleasure. "To Gorebreath, then."

The path wriggled again, but Gubble stepped heavily on the end to hold it down.

"No wiggle!" he instructed. The path responded with a sharp twist that left the troll lying flat on his back with his legs in the air. "Bad path. Path is rude," he grunted as he began to struggle to his feet. "Rude, rude, rude!"

The path quivered gleefully, but as Marcus seated himself, it lay still. "I'll see you very soon, Gracie," he said. "And thanks for the supper. It was brilliant!" He hesitated, wondering if he should kiss her or at least give her a parting hug. He half got up, and at the same moment Gracie leaned toward him to say good-bye.

"Go on, Mr. Prince!" Alf, horrified by the lack of romance, zoomed down with a loud squeak. His arrival startled them both, and Marcus slipped as Gracie lost her balance. The path did a double flip, then swirled away from the house, through the gate, and into the midst of the forest that surrounded the House of the Ancient Crones. Marcus, all breath knocked out of him by the speed with which they were switchbacking in and out of the trees, decided the only thing to do was to shut his eyes tightly and hope for the best. This had the curious effect of sending him to sleep, and when the path finally stopped with an abruptness that sent him slithering to the ground, he woke with a start and looked up at the palace walls in astonishment. "Wow! Am I home already?"

The Ancient One, assuming that Gracie would see Marcus off and then finish up washing the dishes, returned to the looms in room seventeen. There she found Elsie, her wig of tumbling red curls slipping over her nose, in the middle of an argument with Foyce.

"It's no good," Elsie was saying. "You can't expect Prince Albion to accept a cloak covered in butter. You'll have to unravel that whole section."

Foyce was at the point of refusing to do anything of the sort when she saw Edna's cold blue eye watching her. Grumbling, she sat herself in front of the loom.

"So I should hope," Edna said sharply. "And we'll have no more of that kind of behavior, thank you. Val, shall I take a turn at the web of power?"

The Youngest was frowning at the fine silvery fabric in front of her. "I can't quite make it out," she said. "Sometimes I think it's perfectly smooth, and sometimes there seems to be a kind of roughness, although I don't think it's anything to worry about."

Edna bent to inspect the web, and Elsie came to stand beside her. "Hmm. I see what you mean." The Ancient One ran a gnarled finger over the quivering material on the loom. "I'd say whatever's causing this is a long way off. It's certainly not in the Five Kingdoms. It could be as far away as the Outer Mountains."

"The dragons?" Val suggested. "Could they be up to something? Or the giants?"

Elsie snorted. "The giants? They haven't moved a step for at least a hundred years. Much more likely to be some kind of Dark Magic."

Edna was looking thoughtful. "Possibly. Still, there's no discoloration. None at all. So whatever it is can't be dangerous, or at least it won't be endangering the Five Kingdoms." She sighed and sat down in the large armchair beside the loom. "We'll just keep an eye on it. Elsie dear, perhaps you'd like to help Foyce?"

Foyce, who had unraveled no more than three lines of the scarlet cloth, hastily covered the remaining butter stains with her handkerchief and began to weave as fast as she could go. Elsie gave the handkerchief a suspicious glare, but before she could make any comment, there was a loud squeaking and a bat zigzagged in through the window.

"*Ciao!* Greetings! And a very good evening to all and sundry. Anyone seen my nephew?"

"Hello, Marlon." Elsie smiled as the bat landed neatly on the curtain rail. "Alf was here a few minutes ago. Do you need him urgently?"

Marlon scratched his ear. "Nah. Just wondering." He peered around the room. "Where's the kid?"

"Gracie?" The Ancient One looked up. "She's saying good-bye to Marcus. Or else she's in WATER WINGS."

Marlon shook his head. "Checked. Nobody there."

Edna's one eyebrow rose. "Really? And she wasn't outside?"

Marlon shook his head again. "*Nada*. Nothing. No path either, come to think of it."

"Well, that makes sense," Edna told him. "It's taken Prince Marcus back to Gorebreath."

"Maybe the kid went too," Marlon suggested.

The Ancient One frowned. "Marcus needed to speak to his parents. And Gracie would never do such a thing without telling us first. Did you see Gubble?"

Marlon shook his head, and the Ancient One hauled herself out of her chair. She was beginning to have a niggling feeling that all was not well, but her voice was calm as she remarked, "He's probably in his cupboard. I suggest we ask him where Gracie is."

But Gubble's cupboard was empty.

Far away, on the other side of the Five Kingdoms, Marcus blinked. He rubbed his eyes and looked again. "Hang on a moment! This isn't Gorebreath! It's—at least I think it is—Albion's place! Hey, Path! Here! Come back!" But the path was gone.

"Ug," said a voice close beside him. "Ug."

"Marcus," asked a second voice, "where are we?"

Chapter Six

Marley Bagsmith had a headache. A bad headache. And worse than the headache was the sickening feeling of having made a mistake—the kind of mistake that has terrible consequences. As he crawled into bed, he came to the worrisome conclusion that he had, while under the influence of strong ale, made a promise of some kind. Exactly what or to whom, he couldn't remember; all he knew for certain was that it was a promise that should never have been made. He groaned, rubbed his aching eyes, and did his best to review the events of the afternoon and evening.

After his meeting with Prince Albion, Marley had set off for Gorebreath with every intention of mingling with the crowd and noting down the celebratory activities, but the knowledge that he had gold and silver in his pocket had proved too much for him. He had twitched and fidgeted all through Prince Arioso's speech, and the distraction caused by Marcus's speedy exit had offered an opportunity he was unable to resist. He had slipped out of the council chamber and left the palace as fast as his legs could carry him, and within minutes was heading in the direction of the Howling Arms. A couple of hours later, a generous distribution of cash had made him remarkably popular with the Howling customers, who were, without exception, lacking in any kind of respectability. Most of them were also lacking funds, so Marley speedily acquired a number of excellent friends who were more than willing to raise their glasses and toast him just as long as he footed the bill. By the end of the afternoon, they were singing cheery songs of eternal brotherhood with a werewolf who had sneaked in through the back door—a door that led to the wilderness on the other side of the border fence.

The inn had been built, if such a ramshackle building could ever be described as having been built, on top of the boundary; a thick white line drawn on the floor of the main drinking area showed where the civilized Five Kingdoms gave way to the unknown and uncivilized lands beyond. It was, however, much more than a mere chalk mark. Deep witches, full-blooded zombies, and werewolves, all forbidden by law to leave the wilderness, kept themselves well away from it. Any attempt to cross to the other side resulted in a sharp stinging sensation followed by an acute and agonizing pain in the head. The stinging sensation was due to the ancient enchantments that protected the Five Kingdoms from evil; the pain in the head was provided by the landlord. Any illegal crossing of the line would result in the loss of his license and the immediate closure of the Howling Arms, so a large and heavy club was permanently on display by the bar. It was no secret that Gruntle Marrowgrease took much pleasure in using the club, and he and the law were treated with a grudging respect.

"We'll alwaysh be friendsh together!" Marley sang. He waved his tankard under the werewolf's nose. "Whether we're sh . . . sh . . . shcary or . . . hairy! Hairy, hairy, ever so sh . . . sh . . . shcary!"

The werewolf let out a low growl, and Marley blinked at it. "Washa matter, my furry friend? Have another drink! The drinksh are all on me!"

The landlord, a very large man with such extensive whiskers that it was obvious to all but the seriously befuddled that he himself was of werewolf ancestry, lifted Marley by the elbows and deposited him in a corner. "Now, now," he admonished, "you be careful with your language, Mr. Bagsmith!" He jerked a thumb in the direction of the werewolf. "You don't want to be upsetting the likes of that. Holds their grudges, they do. You sit yourself down here nice and quiet, and wait until he's gone. He'll be off before long. Full moon tonight, so he'll need to go about his business."

The landlord was right. Hardly ten minutes had passed before the werewolf left as silently as he had come, but Marley did not notice. He was otherwise engaged. What he assumed to be his shadow had developed a curious tendency to swirl around his feet, then creep up and slither rather too tightly around his neck. He flailed and swore at it until Gruntle saw what he was doing and raised a threatening fist.

"Oi!" he growled. "That's one of my best customers! Leave him alone!"

Marley's jaw dropped as he stared blankly at the landlord. "Eh?"

Gruntle pointed at the shadow, which had detached itself and was tiptoeing across the filthy rush-strewn floor toward the bar. "That there's Fiddleduster Squint's shadow, and nobody here goes messing with it. Ain't that right, Mr. Shadow?"

The shadow was now sitting on a bar stool, but it turned and nodded. "Beer," it whispered. "Beer!"

Marley Bagsmith shut his eyes tightly, then opened them again. The shadow was still there, holding a full tankard of Howling Arms' Ale. There was a second tankard on the bar beside it. For a moment, Marley wondered if he was expected to join the shadow for a convivial drink, but before he could move, the back door swung open and the tallest, thinnest man he had ever seen came striding in, settled himself beside the shadow, and downed the ale in one long swallow. Marley clapped in admiration, and the tall man swung around to inspect him.

"Who do we have here, Marrowgrease?"

The landlord shrugged. "Marley Bagsmith, Mr. Squint. Got a pocketful of money for once, and he's here to spend it. Been singing merry ditties, he has, but I popped him in the corner as he was in danger of upsetting a customer. Taken a drink too many, I'd say. Best left to cool off a bit."

"Drink too many? Whatsh that?" Marley, red in the face with indignation, stomped out of his corner. "Never upshet anyone, I didn't. Was having a jolly little shingshong with my friends when that man"—he waved an inaccurate finger in the vague direction of the landlord— "took me away. Not nice. Not hosh . . . hosh . . . hospitabubble. No. And . . ." A sense of injustice combined

with too much alcohol pushed Marley into indiscretion. "And I'm not nobody no more. Not . . . not at all. I'm a . . ." He tapped his nose twice and winked heavily. "A shpy! I mean, spy! Prince Albion's very own spy, I am, so don't YOU go mesh . . . mesh . . . messing with ME!" He smiled the triumphant smile of a man who knows he has had the last word and thunked his empty tankard on the bar to emphasize his point.

"Really?" Fiddleduster's eyes were so dark they looked like hollows in his skull-like face. "A spy? You? What a very surprising and rather distressing thought. How standards must have slipped in Cockenzie Rood."

"But I am!" Marley's bravado was beginning to ebb away under the cold gaze of the emaciated figure in front of him, but he was determined to prove his new status. "Prince Albion told me all sorts of things, secret-like. He said the celebration is going to be different this year, 'cause he's in charge. There's going to be a parade, see. And a talent competition. With prizes. And I'm going to tell him what they did in Gorebreath so we're going to be better than them. Cockenzie Rood forever and all that. So you see, I AM a spy!"

There was a faint flicker in Fiddleduster Squint's eyes, but no reaction other than the slightest raise of an eyebrow.

Gruntle Marrowgrease leaned over the bar top. "Doubt he'd have had the cash if he wasn't up to something, Mr. Squint, sir."

Marley Bagsmith shivered. An uncomfortable sensation was seeping into his consciousness. It was a moment before he recognized it as fear: a deep chilling fear that made his stomach churn and his mouth go dry. He swallowed and did his best to retain a little dignity. "See? Our jolly landlord's a fellow with a bit of sense. And now, if you'll excuse me, I'll go and join my friends." He jingled the remaining coins in his pocket. "Time for another round." And he scuttled away to where Weasel Canker and his associates were lifting their glasses and toasting petty theft, larceny, and good strong beer.

"So we have a royal spy in our midst." Fiddleduster cracked his bony knuckles. "How too, too interesting. And there's to be a talent competition in Cockenzie Rood, with prizes. What kind of prizes, one wonders? But forget the prizes. Just to win would mean recognition — recognition for me and my kind. Gruntle!"

"Yes, sir?" Gruntle stood up straight.

"Allow this Bagsmith all the ale he can drink. And a little more besides, if you would be so kind. I have had an idea." The hollow eyes were alight with a dark enthusiasm. "The Kingdom of Cockenzie Rood is looking for talent, he says. Well, I have talent. I am talented to my fingers' ends. Is that not true, my dear Gruntle?"

A range of expressions flitted across the landlord's face. Beginning with unadulterated horror, it switched to amazement, followed by incredulity, and ended with a synthetic rictus grin. "Absolutely, Mr. Squint, sir. Talented. Yes. Yes, indeed."

Fiddleduster Squint glanced across to where Marley was lolling over a table, staring into the bottom of his glass. "A full measure for Mr. Bagsmith, if you please."

"Of course, milord. Erm . . . is that FREE ale?"

"You told me he had coins in his pocket. Allow him to spend them. And, Gruntle?" Fiddleduster raised an imperious hand. "Give him full measures. None of your watery pints for my very dear friend."

Gruntle Marrowgrease was too much in awe of the cadaverous figure in front of him to raise any objection to this slur on the quality of his ale. Had it been any other customer, he would have spat in their glass before pulling the next pint, but he was uncomfortably aware that the shadow was watching his every move. "Of course, sir," he agreed, and Marley was served without protest.

"Mr. Squint says as you can drink as much as you like," Gruntle told him. "Lucky, you are. Looks like he's taken a liking to you." He leaned over Marley's shoulder and lowered his voice. "A word in your ear. He may have a notion to play his fiddle. Best if you pretend to like it."

Marley was more than happy to agree, but for the moment the tall figure seemed intent on his beer. From time to time, he looked around as if he were checking on the company; when the back door opened with a rush of chilly air, Fiddleduster jumped to his feet. "My dear cousins! Come in, come in! Allow me to present the very honorable Marley Bagsmith, spy to the royal family of Cockenzie Rood!"

The alcohol had dulled Marley's brain, but he was still aware that his position was not one he wished to be advertised to all and sundry. He opened his mouth to protest, but at that moment Fiddleduster's friends came limping, hobbling, and swaying into the room. With them came a strong smell of damp earth, rotting mushrooms, and mold, and the temperature dropped by several degrees. Marley gulped and took a long swig of sustaining beer. The suspicion that Fiddleduster Squint was of zombie ancestry, if not of full blood, had already occurred to him, but there was no doubt at all about the new arrivals. Their clothes hung in tatters about them, and their eyes bulged in their fleshless skulls. It was also noticeable that they, like Fiddleduster, kept well clear of the white line delineating the border of the Five Kingdoms.

"Mucus, Mildew, and Corruption," Fiddleduster announced. "And now my beloved relatives are here, I shall take up my bow. The time has come to delight the ears of all who listen, to soothe the inner soul, to turn the Howling Arms into a sanctuary of sweet music." With a grandiloquent flourish, he pulled a small fiddle out from under his long black coat. "Let me not keep Mr. Bagsmith waiting any longer! I shall begin with 'Lament for a Dead Hedgehog.'"

An ear-splitting screech began, a sound that Marley could only equate with knives being scraped across a plate or fingernails on a blackboard. He shut his eyes, but it made no difference. His mind was jumbled and jangled by the noise, but gradually this jangling was replaced by a terrifying numbness where every thought took an immense effort to follow through from beginning to end. He opened his eyes and made a desperate attempt to rise from his seat, but a swift tap from Fiddleduster's bow put him back in his place.

"Surely you aren't thinking of leaving us so soon, Mr. Bagsmith," Fiddleduster murmured, and the implied menace in his voice made Marley shake his head. A moment later he found himself holding yet another full tankard. By the time he had drained it to the dregs, his brain was empty, apart from a vague idea that all was not well with the world.

The beer continued to flow; the music grew louder and louder. One by one, Marley's drinking companions made their excuses until only the zombies were left, staring at Marley as he sat slumped in his chair, eyes glazed. Fiddleduster Squint, never ceasing to play, watched him with a constant and calculating gaze. It was only when he judged the moment was exactly right that he stepped to Marley Bagsmith's side, the final despairing notes of "The Hammering of the Slug" still lingering in the air.

"A fine rendition," he remarked, "as I'm sure you'll agree, Mr. Bagsmith?"

Marley waved a feeble arm.

"Would you not say, Mr. Bagsmith, that my music would make an excellent addition to any talent competition?"

The zombies clapped their bloodless hands, and Marley beamed a meaningless smile.

"Oh, yesh," he agreed. "Show . . . show . . . kick, kick . . . show . . ."

"What a very perceptive and intelligent man you

are, Mr. Bagsmith," Fiddleduster purred. "So you'll accept my application? No entry forms needed, no documentation required? And safe passage across the border included, of course. You can easily secure me an invitation, I have no doubt. A written invitation, so there can be no confusion with those foolish border guards." An expression of extreme malevolence flitted across his bony face. "Such prejudice. Such animosity! 'Zombies! Zombies? But we can't POSSIBLY allow those nasty zombies in our dear sweet, smug little kingdoms.'" His voice lost its mocking tone, and he turned back to his companion. "Oh, how too, too wonderful to have a friend in such high places as your good self!" He seized Marley's hand and pressed it in gratitude. "You agree? One has your promise?"

Marley, lost in a swirling mist of alcoholic well-being, was brought back to earth with a bump. It felt as if his hand was being grasped by a bunch of icy twigs, and he looked down in shocked surprise. "Agree? Yush. Yuss . . . anything you shay . . . OUCH!"

His hand was released, and Fiddleduster swung around to his shadow. "Shadow? A little task for you, dear fellow. Keep our good friend Mr. Bagsmith close company. Remind him, should he need it, of his promise." He waved his fiddle bow in farewell. "Pray excuse me, Mr. Bagsmith. I must head for the wilderness. The moon will be high, and I have work to do. Late travelers await my music. I must stir their hearts and send them dancing down the road rejoicing." And with one last wave, Fiddleduster Squint followed his hideous cousins out of the back door and was gone.

Gruntle Marrowgrease leaned over the bar. "Time for you to be off, Bagsmith. You've spent your money, and if you ask me — which you ain't, but I'll give you my opinion for free all the same — you've bought a whole lot more than you bargained for."

Marley, his head already beginning to throb, hauled himself out of his chair. "G'night," he said thickly, and set out in the opposite direction from Fiddleduster Squint.

"It must have been a nightmare. A horrible nightmare." Marley spoke out loud as he turned and twisted in his bed. "I always did get the nasties after too much drink. It'll all seem better in the morning." And he lifted himself up to blow out his candle.

"Oh, but it won't, Mr. Bagsmith . . ." The whisper was faint but very clear. "In the morning you must see to your promise. You remember that promise, don't you, Mr. Bagsmith?"

Marley's bloodshot eyes widened in terror. Fiddleduster Squint's shadow was quivering on his ceiling in amongst the loops and trails of cobweb. "Oh, yes . . ." he said. "I remember . . ."

"One is very glad to hear it." The shadow spread its dark spidery arms from one side of the small dingy room to the other, and Marley shuddered. He had spun himself into a web from which even his devious mind could see no way of escaping.

"I'll remember," he repeated, his voice hoarse. "But just leave me alone."

"Oh, no." The shadow shook its head, and the candle flame dipped. "This one will be here all night long, Mr. Bagsmith. This one will be waiting for you . . . waiting for the morning."

Marley gave a loud wail and hid his head under the blankets. The shadow shook with silent laughter before swooping into a dusty corner, where it settled itself for what remained of the night. Marley, trembling, gradually dropped into a restless sleep filled with voices exhorting him to "Remember, Mr. Bagsmith, remember."

Chapter Seven

"GRACIE!" Marcus stared. "What on earth are you doing here?"

Gracie shook her head. She was still feeling confused after the speed of their journey, a journey she had never expected to make. She was also uncomfortably aware that she was wearing an old grubby apron that had seen better days. Looking down, she saw she was still wearing a pair of Auntie Val's hand-me-down bedroom slippers, and her embarrassment grew.

"I don't know. I must have fallen on the path just as you were leaving. Oh!" A sudden recollection came to her. "I remember! Alf made me lose my balance! He was fluttering under my nose."

"Ug." Gubble nodded. "Was bat. Bad bat." He pointed upward. "Him!"

Alf, balanced on a windowsill, did his best to look outraged. "I never, ever did! Would I do such a thing, Miss Gracie? Mr. Prince?"

"Yes." Gracie and Marcus spoke together, and Gubble joined in with a loud affirmative "UG!"

"Well . . ." Alf fluttered his wings. "It's good to have company, isn't it, Mr. Prince? Especially Miss Gracie. I mean, if you're about to go on an adventure, you should be together—"

"But he's not on an adventure!" Gracie snapped, and immediately felt guilty for being cross. She was wishing she was anywhere other than outside a royal palace; Marcus's royal connections made her self-conscious at the best of times, and this was most certainly not one of the best. "Marcus is on his way to see his parents. Aren't you, Marcus?"

Marcus didn't answer. He was staring at the palace walls. "It's definitely Albion's place. What time do you think it is? Shall we pop in and pay a surprise visit?"

Gracie twisted her hands together. "Um," she began. "What about your parents?"

Her companion shrugged. "I'll never get back to Gorebreath in time to see them tonight. The path's gone, and Glee's at your house." Then, seeing Gracie's anxious expression, he added, "Tell you what, why don't we ask Albion if we can borrow a horse? If we gallop all the way, we'd just about be back before Mother and Father go to bed, and I'll tell them how sorry I am, and then you can stay overnight, and we'll go back to your place tomorrow!"

"Gubble? Gubble come too?" The troll tugged at Marcus's sleeve.

Marcus looked at the solid green figure of the troll. "Hmm. Maybe we'd better ask Albion if we can borrow a carriage."

"That sounds like a good idea." Gracie nodded, relieved that the visit to the Royal Palace of Cockenzie Rood was likely to be a brief one. A further thought struck her. "Oh! Poor Auntie Edna! She'll be wondering where I've gotten to! Alf—here's a job for you. You can fly straight back to the crones and tell them what happened." She gave the small bat a hard stare. "EXACTLY what happened, mind you. And give them my love, and say I'm so sorry and that I'll be home very soon."

Alf drooped. "It's been a long day, Miss Gracie."

"I'm sure the aunties will look after you. Now, GO!" Gracie sounded unusually forceful, and Alf spread his wings in readiness for takeoff.

"I'll be on my way." He flew a swift circle over

Gracie's head. "Even though you haven't said thank you, Miss Gracie."

"Thank you?" Gracie looked at Alf in astonishment. "Why should I thank you? If it wasn't for you, I wouldn't even be here!"

The little bat waved a claw. "But you and Mr. Prince are together again!" And then he was gone.

Marcus overheard Alf's final remark but ignored it. He had realized that Gracie wasn't entirely happy, but he had no idea why. Aprons and bedroom slippers meant nothing to him; as far as he was concerned, Gracie was always his very special friend, whatever she was wearing. A vague idea that he might have upset her by arriving so unexpectedly at the crones' house floated into his mind. *Maybe she didn't want to see me?* he wondered as he led the way to the palace front door. It was not a good thought, and he gave Gracie a quick sideways glance. Gracie was worrying about what royalty would think of her down-at-the-heel slippers; her expression was gloomy, and Marcus was not reassured. "She's wishing she was at home. Oh, bother! If only today hadn't happened. Just about everything's gone wrong, and now Gracie doesn't want to be here." Taking a deep breath, he became exceedingly brisk to cover up his disappointment.

"Come on! Hurry up! The sooner we see Albion, the sooner we can be on our way."

He strode on ahead, and Gracie looked after him in surprise. "He's ashamed of the way I look," she told herself, and sighed. "I can't say I blame him."

Gubble, who never suffered from any form of introspection, grunted as he did his best to keep up. "Prince walking too fast. Gubble too slow."

Gracie took his arm and drew him into the shadow of the portico. "Here. Look—Marcus is ringing the doorbell! Why don't we stay here while he arranges for the horse and carriage."

Gubble was grateful for any opportunity to catch his breath, and he and Gracie stood still while Marcus waited impatiently outside the gilded front door.

A manservant dressed in velvet and golden lace swung the heavy door open, and the portly and self-important figure of the royal butler stepped out. He inspected Marcus with suspicion. Most visitors to the palace arrived in golden coaches or glittering carriages, or at the very least riding on a well-groomed horse; it was rare, indeed, to find a tousled and dusty young man standing on the doorstep. "Good evening," he said coldly. "Might I ask the nature of this h'unexpected visitation?"

"Hi," Marcus said cheerfully. "Where's Sponge? Are you new? I've not seen you before, have I?"

The butler's eyes narrowed at Marcus's lack of respect. "Mr. Sponge, young man, has gone into retirement. His Majesty has done me the h'enormous honor of appointing me in Mr. Sponge's place. Now, I will ask you again. What is the nature of this visitation? The kitchen door is to be found at the rear of the palace."

Marcus frowned and stood up straight. "I am Prince Marcus of Gorebreath, here to see Prince Albion. Prince Marcus, together with Gracie Gillypot— Gracie? Gracie, where are you?"

Gracie stepped out from the shadows, followed by Gubble. The butler took one look, then folded his arms with an expression of intense disapproval. "I suggest, young man, that you and the young person with the h'unfortunate bedroom slippers take yourselves off and away right now this minute. And make sure you take that . . . that green h'appendage with you. The royal household of Cockenzie Rood is not in the habit of receiving riffraff!" He moved away with the obvious intention of slamming the door but was prevented by a furious Marcus leaping forward and seizing the heavy brass handle.

"Hang on a minute!" The prince's face was beet red. "Call Prince Albion! He'll tell you who I am!"

In reply the butler raised an imperious hand. The manservant pulled a silver whistle from his pocket and blew on it. At once there was the sound of running feet, and four burly soldiers came hurrying from the guardhouse on the other side of the driveway. Marcus, wildly protesting, was picked up by the largest and slung over his shoulder, while another swept Gracie off her feet and tucked her under his arm. The remaining two hesitated. Gubble was growling loudly and swaying from side to side in a menacing fashion.

"Put me DOWN!" Marcus yelled. "Put me DOWN! And put Gracie down too, you big bully! Put her down this minute!"

Gubble growled louder and took a step forward. The soldiers took a step back.

"NO, Gubble!" Gracie shouted as she was carried bodily down the steps. "NO! Run away! Oh, do run away!"

The troll blinked at her. "Gubble run? Gubble run where?"

Before Gracie could answer, the two soldiers seized their chance. Grabbing Gubble by the arms, they lifted him high off the ground and began marching him in the direction of the guardhouse. "We'll lock it in for the night," said the tallest. "'Orrible creature. Thought trolls were banned."

"Don't worry, Gubble!" Gracie had seen what was happening but was unable to do anything to help. "We'll get you out! Just be good! It's all a terrible mistake!"

"Suggest you keep quiet too, miss," said her captor. "Oi! Captain! What do we do with the girl?"

The captain of the guard was carrying Marcus, who had not stopped kicking and squirming and shouting for an instant. The captain's back and shoulders were battered and bruised, and his helmet was over one eye. "This one needs teaching a lesson," he grunted. "We'll put him in the lockup for the night. If the troll gives him a chew or two, it's no more than what he deserves. Let the girl go, but see she takes herself off the property. Village kid, most likely, come to gawp at 'is Highness. No manners, these days. None at all!"

The butler had been watching Marcus and Gracie's capture with approval. Rubbing his hands together, he remarked, "That young fellow had the h'audacity to h'inform me that he was a prince. Did you ever hear the like?"

"Blooming outrage!" The captain puffed out his cheeks. "Don't think he was after the silver, do you?"

The butler paused to consider. "It seems h'unlikely that a burglar would come knocking at the front door," he said, with some regret. "No. My h'opinion is that he is what I would refer to as a chancer. Put him in the lockup, Captain."

"Let me GO!" Marcus bellowed. "Let me see Albion! Or the duchess! Or King Dowby—"

The captain clapped a firm hand over Marcus's mouth and marched him across the road. A moment later he was pushed into a small windowless cell smelling strongly of cold, wet stone, troll, and disinfectant. Dumped unceremoniously on the floor, Marcus heard the door being bolted not once, but three times. Then came the sound of a shouted order and departing footsteps, followed by silence.

There was a stirring in the darkness, and the clank of chains. "Is Gracie?" asked a hopeful voice.

Chapter Eight

The path had not returned to the House of the Ancient Crones, there was no sign of Alf, and Gracie was, without a doubt, missing. Val was already fearing the worst and alternated wiping her eyes with blowing her nose on a large pink handkerchief. Elsie had pulled at the curls of her wig until she resembled a ginger dandelion. "It just isn't like her to vanish without leaving a message," she said.

"You've said that three times already," Foyce pointed out. "I'd say the brat's done run off with her boyfriend. Who'd want to stay here if they didn't have to?" Elsie shot her a sharp look, and Foyce went back to her weaving, muttering to herself. "Was just saying. Didn't mean any harm."

"That may be," Elsie snapped. "If you want to leave here, my girl, you'll have to change your attitude. And you've got a long way to go, let me tell you."

The Ancient One was studying the web of power. "Hush, Elsie. I know you're worried, but there's no need to take it out on Foyce. Gracie's a Trueheart; whatever she's doing, she'll have our protection. And there's no sign of evil in the kingdoms." She went on staring at the web. "But there's something niggling at the back of my mind. Nothing to do with Gracie. Mmmmm . . . Elsie, what was it you said earlier? You said something about the giants?"

"Did I?" Elsie looked blank. She took off her wig and rubbed at her bald head. "Oh. I remember now. It was nothing. Just that they won't be causing any trouble. They haven't moved an inch for ages."

Edna's gaze intensified. "No! You said they hadn't moved for at least a hundred years! THAT was what was troubling me. They must be due to move, and that's always been, shall we say, interesting in the past. Of course, they may decide to move in the opposite direction, away from the kingdoms. We can but hope. The last time they moved, they caused a tidal wave on Howling Mere, and half the population of Cockenzie Rood were flooded out of their houses."

Foyce looked up from the scarlet cloth on her loom. "A hundred years ago? How old ARE you?"

"Older than my teeth, but the same age as my tongue, Miss Inquisitive." The Ancient One ran a finger over the web. "Yes . . . I can definitely feel a stirring . . ."

She was distracted from any further comment by Marlon. He had taken off to investigate the outside of the house in case there were any clues to explain Gracie's disappearance, but now he flew in through the window. "Path's back," he announced. "Looks a bit sorry for itself. You'd better come and see."

Leaving Val and Foyce in room seventeen, Elsie and Edna hurried to the front door. There was no sign of the path.

"Skulking around the corner," Marlon reported from above.

The two crones followed him and found the path doing its best to tie itself up in knots and hide beneath the henhouse.

"It's ashamed of itself," Edna pronounced. "Something's gone wrong." She bent down and peered under the shed. "Come along out, dear. No one's going to hurt you. And we all make mistakes sometimes. Is that why you're hiding? Because you made a mistake?"

The path gave a faint ripple.

Elsie started to say something, but the Ancient One hushed her with a wave of her hand. "Did you take Gracie as well as Marcus?"

The ripple was more pronounced.

"I see." Edna creaked upright. "I thought as much."

"Did you take Gubble too?" Elsie wanted to know. "And Alf?"

The path rippled again but still showed no sign of emerging. The chickens flapped encouragement, but the path ignored them.

Marlon flew a swift circle. "Not my speciality," he remarked, "but I'd say you ain't heard the half of it. Kid was headed for Gorebreath, did you say?"

Edna and Elsie nodded, and the path turned a deep guilty pink.

"Gotcha," Marlon said triumphantly. "There's the story. Wrong place." He flew lower. "Am I right, or am I right?"

The path gave a feeble wriggle of assent, and Edna frowned. "Oh, dear. But you did go to one of the Five Kingdoms?"

At once the path threw off its knots and came sliding out from under the henhouse, wriggling cheerfully.

Elsie wagged a reproachful finger. "Bad path! Poor

Gracie. No wonder we couldn't find her. Still, I'm sure Marcus'll look after her."

Marlon made another circle. "Niven's Knowe?" he asked. "Dreghorn? Wadingburn?"

The path took no notice.

"Where have I forgotten? Yeah. Cockenzie Rood?"

There was a guilty twitch, and the bat flew a victory roll. "Result. I'll be offski. Gonna check it out!" And he was gone.

"Bother." The Ancient One turned to go back into the house. "I wanted to ask him if he'd heard any rumors about the giants."

"I'm sure it'll all be fine." Elsie fell in to step beside her. "And if it isn't, we'll hear soon enough. Or the web will tell us."

The Ancient One sighed. "You're quite right, Elsie dear. And we've still got five of those cloaks to finish."

As they walked back into the house, the path gave a long shudder of relief. Noticing that it was beginning to rain, it looped itself around and sank back into its usual position between the front door and the gate that led out into the Less Enchanted Forest. There it lay still, only a very occasional twitch suggesting that it might, just possibly, be considering other options.

Chapter Nine

Prince Albion was admiring himself in a mirror. His military uniform was a triumph, he decided. The grand parade would certainly be the stunning success he had planned, especially if the smart red cloaks for the palace guards were ready in time.

"Must send a message to those creepy weaving women," he told himself. "Tell them to hurry up. Aha! I know. I'll get . . . What was his name, now? That spy fellow . . . Bill. Bill something. I'll get him to see to it tomorrow."

Pleased with this idea, Albion adjusted the scarlet plume on his hat and saluted his reflection. "Guard! ATTEN . . . SHUN! Guard! AT . . . EASE!" A self-congratulatory twirl reminded him that he was now in possession of a ceremonial sword, and his smile grew wider. Pulling it from its sheath, he waved it in the air.

"Die, villain, die!" he shouted, and lunged at his pillows. A moment later the room was filled with flying feathers. Prince Albion coughed, then panicked. His beautiful new uniform had turned snowy white, and as fast as he brushed the feathers away, more floated down. With a cry of despair, he rushed out the door, shouting loudly for help.

"What is it, Albion?" The dowager duchess arrived at the other end of the corridor, looking singularly unconcerned. Albion's panics were legendary and were rarely of any consequence. "Goodness! What a mess! What have you been doing?"

Albion was dancing up and down, flailing at the feathers. "It's ruined!"

"Nonsense," Hortense said sharply. "Stand here, and I'll send your valet up with a brush. Then come down for dinner." She looked rather more closely at her nephew. "Is that some kind of uniform?"

"What?" Albion suddenly remembered his uniform was meant to be a secret. If his aunt put two and two together, she might suspect his wonderful plans for a parade on Cockenzie Rood Day, and there was little doubt she would forbid it. "No, no." He waved a casual arm, sending feathers fluttering. "It's just something

I found . . . in the nursery. Yes. The dress-up box, don't you know. Super-duper stuff in there, but a bit mothy." He sneezed loudly, and yet more feathers whirled about his head. "Better get changed. See you at dinner, cuz." And he popped back into his bedroom like a rabbit bolting into its hole.

Hortense, still curious about Albion's appearance, was about to follow him, but she was distracted by the sound of shouting outside the palace. *Strange*, she thought, and went to look, but by the time she reached a window facing the right direction, there was no sign of any unusual activity. One soldier was locking up the guardhouse for the night, and another couple were engaged in animated conversation with Bullstrop, the new butler.

Humph! Hortense thought. *Bullstrop's duties are meant to be inside the palace, not outside. Still . . . maybe he went out for a breath of fresh air.* And she swept away to give instructions to Prince Albion's valet before making her way down the grand staircase to the enormous and over-furnished dining room, where the table was laid for three. Of King Dowby, however, there was no sign.

When Albion came down to dinner, he was dressed in his usual style, apart from a couple of feathers in his hair. His valet had managed to restore the uniform to its previous pristine condition, and the prince had taken the precaution of swearing him to secrecy with the promise of chocolates and an extra day off.

"Looks like splendid soup, cuz," he said as he sat himself down. "Simply splendid!"

"Thank you, Albion." The duchess stirred her own soup thoughtfully. "Do you know anything about Bullstrop? The new butler? Where did he come from?"

"Oh!" Albion looked relieved. He had been worrying about an interrogation on the subject of his uniform. "Pa appointed him. He was Pa's coachman, but he kept getting such terrible chilblains, he couldn't get his boots on, so Pa said he'd be better off working inside." Albion giggled. "He's a bit of a change from Sponge, isn't he?"

Hortense thought fondly of the kind and venerable Sponge, who had played bears with a very young Albion for hours on end with never a word of complaint. "He is, indeed."

"Quite smart, though. Gives a good impression. Sponge was—well, a bit faded around the edges." Albion attacked his soup with vigor. "And it's good for Cockenzie Rood to be up-to-date in every way."

"Hmm," the duchess said doubtfully. "That's a matter of opinion. Is your father coming in for dinner?"

Albion shook his head. "I saw him this afternoon.

He's gone to a horse fair. Won't be back for—" The prince stopped himself just in time. He had been thrilled to the core by the news that his father was going to be away for a whole week, including Cockenzie Rood Day. So thrilled, in fact, that he had omitted to remind the king that the duchess was also intending to be away. When King Dowby said, "Cousin Hortense'll run everything. She always does, always will, so I might as well leave her to it," Albion had merely nodded. He had justified his action by telling himself he had not told a lie. He had merely taken a decision to avoid unnecessary explanations.

He smiled at the duchess and amended his statement to "Pa said he'd be back very soon."

"Good," said the duchess. "As long as he's back in time to make his speech. Now, dear, tell me. Did you hear a disturbance earlier this evening?"

Albion looked blank. "Disturbance?"

Hortense nodded. "Shouting. Outside the front door."

Albion continued to look blank. "No," he said. "I didn't hear anything. Can I have some more soup?"

Hortense rang the bell. A moment later Bullstrop oozed his way into the dining room.

"You rang, Your Grace?"

"The prince would like more soup, if you please,"

the duchess told him. "And, Bullstrop, what was going on earlier this evening? I heard shouting, and shortly afterward I caught sight of you outside in conversation with some of the guard."

Bullstrop smiled an oily smile. "I do hope you weren't h'unduly disturbed, Your Grace. It was merely a couple of foolish young vagrants and a green h'object taking h'advantage of the open h'approach to the palace. The young man became h'abusive, Your Grace, and had to be forcefully suppressed. The h'object has been dealt with. You will not be bothered again."

"A green object?" The duchess's eyebrows rose. "What kind of green object? Do you mean a vegetable?"

Albion dropped his spoon and looked anxious.

Bullstrop coughed. "It was, so to say, Your Grace, a troll."

"A troll?" Hortense, Dowager Duchess of Cockenzie Rood, prided herself on keeping calm in every situation. Nevertheless, her voice rose as she asked, "Are you telling me a troll came knocking on our front door, and nobody thought to tell me?"

The butler grew even more haughty. "It h'appeared to be the property of a young female with h'unfortunate footwear. As such, I judged it h'unnecessary to bother you."

"Quite right!" Albion beamed at Bullstrop.

"Be quiet, Albion," his cousin snapped. "Where is this troll now? And the girl? And what of the young man? Did he also have unfortunate footwear?"

Bullstrop felt himself on firmer ground. "The young man, Your Grace, was singularly h'objectionable. He had the h'audacity to call himself a prince. Prince Marcus, if I remember, and when challenged—"

Albion gave a shriek of laughter. "SUPER-DUPER! It's Marcus and Gracie and that troll—what's he called? Bobble. You thought Marcus was a tramp! Oh, serves him right! Serves him jolly well right! He never ever brushes his hair or polishes his boots, and I don't suppose he washes his neck much either!"

The duchess had risen from her chair. "Am I to understand," she asked, and her voice was icy, "that Prince Marcus and his friends have been locked up?"

Bullstrop folded his arms. "H'excuse me. It was a simple h'error of judgment, Your Grace."

"I see. I have to say that I believe your appointment as butler also to have been an error of judgment. You are dismissed, Bullstrop. Collect your things, and leave the palace. Albion! Stop giggling this instant, and come with me. We must release poor Marcus!"

Chapter Ten

Gracie Gillypot was slowly making her way back toward the Royal Palace of Cockenzie Rood. She had been marched down the palace driveway by one of the soldiers, her slippers flip-flapping as she tried to keep up, and was sent away in the direction of the village.

"Off with you, missie," the soldier said, but not unkindly. "And don't go playing games like that again. If you were wanting a peek at His Highness, you'll see plenty of him on Cockenzie Rood Day." He dropped a meaningful wink. "Got plans, the prince has. Can't tell you no more, but you dress yourself up a bit and get in the front row, and you'll see him good and proper." He winked again, slapped Gracie cheerfully on the back, and stood watching as she trailed away along a path leading to a small cluster of houses.

Gracie, thinking hard, headed for the nearest cottage. It was surrounded by trees and bushes, and as soon as she had reached the shelter of the largest tree, she looked back to see if the soldier had gone. He was standing where she had left him. As she watched, he took off his helmet, scratched his head, put his helmet back on, and sat down on a milestone. He then pulled a pipe from his pocket and, to Gracie's horror, settled himself for a comfortable smoke.

"I'll just have to wait," she told herself. "Oh, I do wish Marlon was here. Or Alf." She leaned against the tree and looked hopefully up into the branches. "Anyone there? Any bats?"

There was no answer.

Gracie began to sigh, then stopped herself. "Come on, Gracie Gillypot! This won't do. Standing here feeling sorry for yourself, and you a Trueheart! You should be pleased you're having an adventure, even if you didn't quite mean to and your slippers keep falling off." She had another quick peek at the soldier; he was now blowing smoke rings. Gracie straightened her shoulders and tied her disreputable apron a little tighter. "As soon as he goes away, I'll get back to the palace. Maybe I should try and find Prince Albion? Hmm." She twisted the end of her braid. "I think I'll find Marcus and Gubble first. Marcus knows far more about palaces than I do."

Satisfied that she had made a sensible decision, Gracie arranged herself so she could watch the soldier without being seen. As the minutes ticked by, she did her best to think Positive and Encouraging Thoughts. "It's no good worrying about Marcus," she told herself. "He probably went marching on ahead like that because . . . because . . . oh, bother. But——" Gracie brightened. "But on the other hand, he did shout at the soldier to put me down. So that's all right." It wasn't, quite, but she resolutely stuck her chin in the air and began to whistle under her breath.

Now, finally, she was retracing her steps. The evening had turned into night, but there were gas lamps flaring on either side of the palace drive. Gracie was doing her best to keep hidden among the ornamental shrubs edging the drive, but it was not easy. Behind the shrubs was woodland, and at every step a twig snapped or leaves rustled, making her jump.

It began to rain: a steady drizzle that trickled down Gracie's neck until she was as wet on the inside of her clothes as on the outside. Her slippers were so sodden, they weighed her down like lead weights. She was tempted to kick them off and go barefoot, but was unsure how she would explain their absence to Auntie Val, who was fond of them.

"Think how pleased Marcus and Gubble will be to see you," she told herself as she struggled on.

A moment later she heard the clatter of hooves. "The guards!" Gracie hurled herself into the depths of the nearest shrub and waited, her heart pounding. It was not, however, the guards. It was a coach traveling at such a speed that Gracie caught only the briefest glimpse of the occupants. She rubbed her eyes. Had she really seen Marcus? Marcus, his face pale in the gaslight, leaning forward as if to urge the driver on? If it was Marcus, then where was Gubble? Gracie shook her head. She must have imagined it. She extricated herself from the bush with some difficulty, but just as she disentangled herself from the last clinging creeper, she heard heavy footsteps coming toward her.

"Oh, BOTHER!" she said. Back into the shrub she went, hoping the rain would disguise any noise she might make, and waited to see who was coming. Even the footsteps sounded angry, and as the bulky figure drew close, Gracie could hear muttering and swearing. To her astonishment, she recognized the butler who had refused to let Marcus into the palace; he was carrying a large suitcase and a bulging leather bag, and his expression made her sink back deeper among the thorns and hold her breath.

Five minutes later she emerged for the second time, not only soaked to the skin but with several painful scratches and leaves in her hair. One of the slippers had disappeared and could not be found; with a certain guilty relief, Gracie abandoned the other one and squelched out onto the edge of the driveway. To cheer herself up, she began talking to herself. "I don't think I really ought to keep hiding away. After all, it isn't as if I've done anything wrong. And neither have Marcus and Gubble. It's all a big misunderstanding. In fact, by now it's probably been sorted out, and Marcus and Gubble are having a good laugh about it with Prince Albion. And maybe even some dinner—oh! Just imagine hot soup! And toast!" Gracie's stomach gave a hungry rumble. "But what time is it?" She squinted into the darkness at the top of the drive. "I can't see any lights on . . ." A hideous premonition floated into her mind. What if she arrived at the palace to find that everyone had gone to bed? What would she do? As her cheery thoughts faded, others took their place. "Marcus can't have gotten free, or he'd have come looking for me . . . wouldn't he? Gubble would. I know he would. So they must be in the guardhouse after all . . . oh, dear." And Gracie wiped her eyes, hoping it was rain and not tears making it so difficult to see.

"Chin up, kiddo!"

"MARLON!" Gracie spun around, her woes forgotten. "Dearest Marlon—where are you?"

"Over here," said the wonderfully familiar voice. "Bit damp tonight. Don't know if you've noticed."

Gracie wiped the rain out of her eyes. "I had, actually. Just a bit. But I can't see you . . ."

"Don't do rain. Only in emergencies. Over here."

Gracie peered upward and saw Marlon hanging from the underside of a gas lamp. What provided shelter for a bat did not do much for Gracie. "Have you been to the palace?" she asked through chattering teeth. "Did you see Marcus and Gubble?"

"Nah. Just arrived. What's up?"

"Oh, Marlon!" Gracie heard her voice wobble and took a deep breath. "Marlon, it's all been horrible. The path brought us here by mistake, and Marcus and Gubble are locked up in the guardhouse—at least, I think they are, but I don't know . . ."

"Never fear, Marlon's here," Marlon said cheerfully. "Keep going, kid. I'll zip ahead and do recon on the joint. See you in five!" And he was gone.

Chapter Eleven

Marcus was fretting. As the coach bumped and rattled its way toward Gorebreath, he shifted from side to side trying to make sense of all that had happened that day. When two red-faced soldiers had unlocked the door of his cramped and uncomfortable prison, his first question had been "Where's Gracie?"

Albion, grinning from ear to ear, had popped up beside them. "Oops! Bit of a boo-boo, Marcus old chap."

"But where's Gracie? Is she here?"

The taller of the two soldiers coughed. "If Your Highness, and apologies for all inconvenience caused, is referring to the young lady, I can report that she is safely restored to her home."

Marcus stared at him. "She's back at home?"

The tall soldier nodded. "Saw her heading up the path with my very own eyes."

Marcus blinked. Had the path come to fetch Gracie? In the strange world of the Ancient Crones, anything was possible. "And . . . and she looked all right? She didn't . . . that is . . . she didn't leave any message, or anything like that?"

The soldier was a kind man. Thinking to make Marcus feel better, he said cheerily, "Not a word. Couldn't wait to get back, I'd say. Skipping along, happy as a lark."

"Oh." Marcus rubbed at his hair. "I see. Look, can you unlock Gubble?"

"Albion?" The duchess appeared in the doorway, still dressed for dinner. "Have you apologized to poor Marcus? And his friends? Marcus, dear boy, I can't tell you how sorry I am that this has happened. What can we do to make it up to you? Do come and have some dinner, and stay the night. We can make you very comfortable."

"Stay the night?" Albion stopped grinning. "Why would he want to stay the night, cuz?"

"Of course he must stay. And . . . What did you say his friends were called? Gracie Gillypot and Mr. Bobble? They must stay too."

Albion made a faint noise of disapproval, and Hortense held up her hand. "Don't be silly, Albion.

You and Marcus have known each other since you were babies. You can have a lovely breakfast together and catch up on old times. Now, I'll go and order more food for everyone, and you bring them to the dining room." And she swept away, leaving Albion opening and closing his mouth while he tried unsuccessfully to think up an objection to his cousin's plans.

"Ug." Gubble came stomping out from the shadows. "Where Gracie?"

"She's gone back to the House of the Ancient Crones," Marcus told him. "The path came to collect her." He turned to the tall soldier. "That's right, isn't it? You saw the path taking her home?"

The soldier looked blank. "Eh?"

Gubble grunted and headed for the door. "Find Gracie," he said. "Gubble find Gracie NOW." With a baleful glare, he elbowed the soldiers out of the way. A moment later he had disappeared into the darkness outside.

"Is he dangerous?" Albion asked anxiously.

Marcus shook his head. "No. Not at all. But he doesn't really listen to anyone except Gracie. He'll be OK. Oh, dear." He looked at Albion. "I didn't mean to arrive out of the blue like this. I meant to go back to Gorebreath, but we ended up here by mistake.

I say, Albion, I'm in terrible trouble with my parents. I don't suppose I could borrow a horse, could I? You see, I really do need to see Father and Mother tonight . . ."

"Going home? You've got to get back to Gorebreath? Tonight?" Even through his confusion, Marcus recognized the relief in Albion's voice. "Of course you can borrow a horse, old boy. Ten horses! Twenty if you need 'em! Leave it to me. I'll get it sorted out. Super-duper!"

And before he could ask any questions, Marcus found himself swept away to the stables, and orders given for the fastest coach to be made ready immediately.

"But I can ride," he protested. "Honestly I can!"

"But if you go now, you can pick up Bobble," Albion told him. "He can't have gone far. Pick him up, and take him with you."

As Marcus swung himself into the coach, a thought occurred to him. "Albion, are you up to something? Something you don't want me to know about?"

"ME?" Albion slammed the coach door shut with a crash. "Planning something? Oh, no, no, no. What could I possibly be planning? Driver, are you ready? Off you go, then! Super-duper! Have a good trip!

Nice to see you! Do come again . . ." Albion waved as the coach bowled out of the stable yard. "But not tomorrow," he added to himself as he marched back to the palace. "Not tomorrow. Tomorrow I have plans." He gave a self-congratulatory chuckle. "Me and my spy."

Now Marcus was looking out the window of the coach, although it was difficult to make out anything more than looming shapes in the darkness. He had little hope of finding Gubble. The troll liked to travel in a direct line, and walls and hedges were no barrier. He simply walked through them. Marcus sighed and wondered for the fiftieth time if Gracie was home by now, and if she was, what she was doing. *Maybe she's really fed up with me,* he thought. *But it just doesn't feel right that she went skipping off and didn't leave a message. She's not like that. Something's wrong somewhere, I know it is . . . but what?* He let out a long, dissatisfied whistle. *Oh, well. I'll sort things out with Father tonight, and then I'll go over to the House of the Ancient Crones tomorrow. I've got to collect Glee, so it won't look odd. And then I can have a chat with Gracie.*

It was all too much. Marcus leaned back against the cushions and drifted into an unsatisfactory sleep filled with the echoes of shouting soldiers and slamming doors. Somewhere in his dreams was Gracie, but was she looking for him or running away?

It was a long night.

The last chimes of midnight found Prince Albion sitting up in bed studying his List of Events for Cockenzie Rood Day, his uniform arranged on a chair close beside him.

"Should I really have the talent competition?" he pondered. "The parade's the thing. Do I really want a whole lot of peasants singing songs about turnips?" He sucked the end of his gold pen. "After all, I'm bound to win it." A feeling of enormous generosity flooded over him. "And as I'm bound to win it, it's a bit unfair to everyone else to let them have a go. Goodness me! I never knew I was so thoughtful!" A smug smile spread over the prince's face. "So there we are. Much better if I cancel it." He drew a thick line through *Tallent Show*. "And what about the choral presentation? I can't conduct in my uniform." He stretched out a hand and lovingly stroked the glittering golden braid on his jacket. "No. We don't need that either. In fact" — the prince gave a small bounce of excitement — "why don't we just have the parade and make it twice as long?"

Theatricale Finale and *Coral Presintation* were struck off with a flourish. "That's the ticket! We'll march around and around, and then I'll inspect the troops, and they can salute me and . . . and then they can fire the cannon in my honor, and I'll bow and everyone will cheer for absolutely AGES! Oh, super-SUPER-duper!" Albion clapped his hands in ecstasy at the thought, and the gold pen rolled off the bed and fell on the floor. The prince took no notice. He threw himself back on his pillows and closed his eyes, his work done. One last thought struck him as he was about to drift into peaceful sleep. "I'll meet that spy fellow, though," he said drowsily. "I'll send him to see the old women. I need those cloaks . . . and a purple velvet cloak for me . . ."

Chapter Twelve

Albion would have been horrified to know that Gracie Gillypot was still within a stone's throw of the palace. She was lying in the middle of a heap of old sacks and looking at a star through a dusty, cobwebbed window.

"You OK, kid?" Marlon asked anxiously. "Not too cold?"

Gracie shook her head. The rain had gradually cleared away as she reached the top of the drive and made her way to the guardhouse. Marlon had already checked it out and found it empty, but Gracie still wanted to look for herself.

"Nobody there, kiddo," Marlon told her. "Quiet as the grave."

Gracie knew he was right, but a small hope that there might be some message, or even a note, made her walk around the solid stone building. There was nothing. Next she turned to look at the palace, but there were no lights in any of the windows.

"I don't think I'd better wake them up," she said. "They don't know me. I mean, I've met Prince Albion a few times, but he always looks at me as if I was a beetle. I don't think he approves of Marcus being my friend."

Marlon made a rude noise. "No brain. Want me to check the kitchens?"

"I'm sure they'll be in bed by now. Maybe there's somewhere dry where I can spend the night, and then I'll go back home tomorrow morning." Gracie yawned. "Can you see anything?"

"Be back soon." Marlon flew higher and circled around. Minutes later he returned, looking pleased with himself. "Vegetable garden," he reported. "Good big shed, sacks inside. And Auntie Vera. Bit of a stick-in-the-mud, but heart in the right place. Says you're welcome!"

Gracie looked surprised. "Auntie Vera? I didn't know you had an aunt."

The bat settled on Gracie's shoulder. "Twenty-seven at the last count. She's the oldest. Knows everything, or thinks she does. Come on, kid. The sooner you get dry, the better."

Gracie, following Marlon's instructions, found the shed easily. The key was in the door, so it was the work of a moment to unlock it, slide inside, and lock herself in. She was greeted by a soft flutter of wings and an exceptionally high-pitched voice encouraging her to make use of the heap of sacks stashed on a low shelf.

"They use them when it's frosty," squeaked Auntie Vera. "But what I say is, if they keep an onion warm, they'll do nicely for a Trueheart. Goodness, child! You're soaked to the skin! Marlon? Out! Let the girl have some privacy."

Now Gracie was warm and dry at last, and her clothes hung dripping from a convenient nail. "Wake me up early," she said sleepily. "I don't want to be discovered by a whole lot of gardeners."

"No prob," Marlon assured her. "Bright 'n' early does it. Sleep well, kiddo."

On the other side of the Five Kingdoms, in Gorebreath, Marcus was staring out his bedroom window, his father's voice still rumbling inside his head. "Disappointment . . . expected better . . . let your brother down . . . embarrassment to us all . . . bad example . . . no support to Arioso . . . spoiled the day . . ."

Marcus opened the window and leaned out to breathe the damp night air. It had been even worse than he had expected, he reflected gloomily. Even his mother had been angry with him. Well, worse than angry. She had cried. Marcus did more deep breathing in the hope of removing the uncomfortable lump in his chest, but it seemed fixed in place.

"Oh, RATS," he said loudly. "So what on earth do I do now? I can't even go and see Gracie. Father'll combust if I'm not around for a day or two. Oh, rats, rats, and double rats! It'll drive me mad." He shut the window with a bang.

The grandfather clock in the House of the Ancient Crones showed half-past two in the morning, but only Foyce was asleep. In room seventeen the looms were busy; Edna was working at the web of power, while Elsie was steadily throwing the shuttle to and fro on the second loom. Val was sitting beside her, stitching at a long red cloak. Alf was balanced on the back of Edna's chair, twittering.

"So all of a sudden, there we were outside the Royal Palace of Cockenzie Rood! You could have knocked me down with a feather! SUCH a surprise for Miss Gracie and Mr. Prince —"

He was interrupted by the Ancient One. "Alf," she said, "you've been talking nonstop for at least half an hour. We're delighted to hear that our girl is safe, and we understand that she slipped onto the path by accident. As did Gubble. And you." She gave the little bat an appraising look with her clear blue eye. "But it seems to me there's something else on your mind. Something you haven't told us yet."

Alf fluttered his wings and hopped from foot to foot. "No, no, no. Well. That is, Miss Gracie did say I should tell you EXACTLY what happened. So I did. I have."

"Really?"

Alf did more hopping and fluttering, but there was no avoiding Edna's steady gaze. "It was just that . . . I mean . . . well, I DID flutter a little bit close to Miss Gracie when she was bending down, and so it's JUST possible that that's why she fell onto the path. If you see what I mean. Are you very angry?"

Edna raised her eyebrow. "Angry? No. Tell me, though. Why—EXACTLY—were you fluttering so close to Gracie?"

The little bat blushed. A rosy glow shone through his fur, and he hung his head. "True romance," he whispered.

"Romance?" Val, needle poised, stared at Alf. "What romance?"

Alf wriggled as hard as if the needle was stuck in his small furry stomach. "Miss Gracie. Mr. Prince. Mr. Prince was going away, see, but Miss Gracie didn't . . . I mean, she wasn't . . ." Totally overcome, Alf flopped onto the floor and crept away to hide his blushes under the heavy wooden loom.

Edna bent down and gently lifted him up. "I think it's you who's the romantic, young Alf," she told him. "But you must listen to me. You can't hurry these things, however much you might wish to. Let Marcus and Gracie work things out for themselves. Now, why don't you have a little sleep, and then you can fly back and tell her everything's fine here, and we'll see her when she gets back. Oh, and you can tell your Mr. Prince that we're looking after his pony too."

Alf yawned an enormous yawn. "It's ever so odd, Mrs. Crone, but I feel so much better now. And I am tired. Ever so tired . . ."

A moment later he was fast asleep in the Ancient One's lap.

Marley Bagsmith tossed and turned all night long, always aware of the dark shadow in the corner. As his room began to lighten with the coming of dawn, he thumped his grubby pillow and decided to give up being a spy. "It's much too much like hard work," he told himself. "Princes. Parades. Competitions! Load of old rubbish."

There was a faint whisper from the corner. "Remember your promise, Mr. Bagsmith . . ."

Marley sat up. "And what if I don't?"

The shadow chuckled. "That would be a mistake. A very bad mistake . . ." A shiver ran up and down Marley Bagsmith's spine. The image of Fiddleduster Squint's cold, fleshless face floated into his mind, and icy-cold fingers squeezed at his stomach.

"Just leave me alone, why can't you?" he wailed. "I'll do what he said. I'll get the prince to let that screeching fiddle player into the competition—" He stopped. The shadow was so close, he could hardly breathe.

"Be careful, Marley Bagsmith. Be careful what you say. My master believes in his music. He has a gift, a gift unrecognized as yet . . . but once it has burst forth upon the Five Kingdoms, all will be changed by him, all will be under his spell."

"Mmmmph!" was all that Marley could manage, but the shadow took this as an apology. It floated back into its corner, and Marley crawled back under his blanket.

The shadow's master was whistling. He had already scared three night travelers up a pine tree and sent an old woman into hiding. She had wandered outside her cottage to look for her cat just as Fiddleduster Squint was passing, and he had immediately offered her an impromptu concert. She was much too deaf to understand his offer, but the wails and shrieks of the fiddle penetrated even her muffled hearing and sent her scuttling for the safety of her closet.

"See, my dears?" Fiddleduster waved his violin bow at his cousins, who had trailed after him for an evening's free entertainment. "See how the beauty of my music renders humans speechless with joy? Oh, I was born for glory. When I am crowned victorious at Cockenzie Rood, my life will truly begin."

Mucus picked a maggot out of his ear. "Begin what, Fiddly Diddly? Scaring cats?"

Fiddleduster Squint frowned. "I will have crossed the border, and what does that mean?"

Mucus looked at Corruption. Corruption looked at Mildew.

"Thunk!" said Mildew.

"Wallop!" said Corruption.

"Thunk, wallop, and ouch from Gruntle's club," Mucus agreed, and all three began to snigger.

"No, no, no." Fiddleduster wagged a long bony finger. "When one is *invited* over the border, one is no longer an outcast. I will be asked to play, and when my music is heard, my power grows. Did you not see how I charmed the Bagsmith to obey my will? And where one has fallen, many will follow. Kings and queens will open their doors and beg me to come in. I will play, and they will surrender their foolish minds to me . . . and I will do as I choose." He gave a high-pitched cackle of laughter. "It might even be that I will open the border to such as you, my dear cousins . . . to you and all others like us!"

Corruption, Mildew, and Mucus came close. "Flesh," they whispered eagerly. "Sweet human flesh?"

"If the border fails," Fiddleduster promised, "the enchantments fail. Each one of us — be we zombies, werewolves, dark witches, or other creatures of the wilderness — is waiting for that time to come . . . And when it does, there will be nothing, nothing to stop us . . ." And he played such a high-pitched celebratory tune on his fiddle that the old woman's cat gave an agonized screech and pulled out all of its whiskers.

*   *   *

The sun was rising as Gubble crashed through a hedge and made his way onto a well-worn track. His face was covered in mud, and a trail of pond weed suggested that his progress had not been straightforward. As the sun broke through the mist, he looked to the left and right, and for the first time since he had left the guardhouse, he hesitated.

"Gubble find Gracie," he muttered. "Ug! Gubble tired." A wooden bench dedicated to the memory of Lodmilla and Turret Witherspoon (*they loved this spot*) caught his eye, and with a grunt he rolled himself underneath. At once his small piggy eyes closed, and he began to snore.

Far, far away, beyond the Wild Enchanted Forest, in a sheltered hollow surrounded by strangely shaped rocks and hillocks, a bird was on the point of bursting into the dawn chorus.

"Tweet!" it began. "Twee—"

The tree it was sitting on trembled, shook, and fell over.

"Awk!" The bird flew high in the air, then headed for the safety of a nearby rock.

The rock gave a deep earthy chuckle.

"WAKE . . . UP," it croaked.

The bird gave a terrified squawk and flew away.

A second rock, covered in lichen, grass, and daisies, stretched itself a couple of yards higher. "NOT . . . LONG . . . NOW."

Chapter Thirteen

Marlon had, without a doubt, meant to wake Gracie early. What he had not anticipated was Auntie Vera wanting to catch up on all the family news and to tell him stories of her twenty-six sisters, their offspring, and their offspring's offspring. It was a very weary bat who finally hung himself up on a roof beam, and the sun was streaming in through the window when he was woken by the sound of footsteps. Gracie had heard them too and was sitting up clutching a sack to her chest. "Is it the gardeners?" she whispered. "Are they coming here?"

Marlon hovered by the window. "Weird-looking guy," he reported. "Sneaky. Up to no good, I'd say—Hang on! What's this?"

Gracie reached for her dress and slid into it. It was still damp but not unbearably so. She left the apron hanging on its nail and tiptoed over to peer out through a dusty pane. "Oh!" She put a hand to her mouth. "That's Prince Albion!"

"And the other guy?" Marlon asked.

"I've never seen him before." Gracie shook her head.

"Looks suspicious to me," Marlon said. "Pin your ears back, kiddo."

Gracie was about to say that she didn't think they should be listening to what was so very evidently a private conversation, but Prince Albion's first words made her gasp and draw nearer to the window.

"House of the Ancient Crones," he said. "Ever heard of it, Bill?"

"Heard of it," Marley Bagsmith said doubtfully. "Best left alone, Your Highness, from all I've heard. Strange goings-on in those there parts. Ouch!"

Albion jumped and looked wildly around. "What? What is it? Is someone about to attack me?"

Marley swallowed nervously. The shadow had slithered under his coat, and after winding itself tightly around his shoulders, was sliding up under his ear. "Remember . . ." it hissed.

"No, no, Your Highness," Marley said. "It was . . . a bee. Or a wasp." He flailed at his head. "Must have stung me. Sorry about that. Erm—about your talent contest—"

"Talent contest?" Albion waved a dismissive hand. "Forget that. I need you to go and see those crones. They're making cloaks for my procession, and they haven't delivered yet. Not good enough, don't you know. Also I need a cloak myself. Purple velvet. Long. You tell them, Bill. Oh, and they could slap on the Cockenzie Rood crest while they're at it. And tell them to hurry!"

Marley's mind was whirling. The shadow was hissing wordlessly in his ear, and his heart was racing. "But, Your Highness! Think . . . think how disappointed your people will be if you don't put on the contest! I mean . . . weren't you going to perform yourself? How sad if we don't get to see you in all your glory!"

"Good!" hissed the shadow. "More! More!"

"And I was at Gorebreath yesterday," Marley went on, his imagination fired by terror. "And everyone there was saying how splendid and . . . and different Cockenzie Rood Day will be, and they were wishing Gorebreath had such a clever and amazing prince to think of such things."

Albion visibly swelled. "Did they? Goodness. Super-duper. Quite right, of course. Quite right."

"And I know of a musician who will make you famous in all the Five Kingdoms," Marley said hurriedly. Seeing the prince's expression, he hastily added,

"Even more famous, that is, than you already are. Extraordinary, he is. He . . . he sounds like nothing you've ever, ever heard—"

Albion hesitated. Surely an extraordinarily talented musician would detract from his own achievements? Or would he be given credit for finding him? The title "Prince Albion, Patron of the Arts," floated attractively in the forefront of his mind.

"Strike now!" hissed the shadow. "Now!"

"He absolutely refuses to go to Gorebreath," Marley wheedled. "He said he wanted to play for Prince Albion of Cockenzie Rood and nobody else, because nobody else was half as important."

Albion began to smile, and Marley waited expectantly. "Excellent," the prince agreed. "Tell him I'll see him today. He can play me a tune or two. If I like him, I'll give him a chance." He drew himself up to his full height of four foot ten. "He can play a tune called . . . called 'An Air for Prince Albion'!"

"Erm . . ." Marley was flummoxed, but the shadow was purring in his ear.

"Well done, Mr. Bagsmith. My master will be delighted." His voice changed to a deeper note. "Once the prince has heard the sweet tunes of my master, all will be arranged to his advantage. Riches will be heaped upon him. Kings and queens will open their doors to him and beg him to come in . . . so my master tells me." The shadow shook its head as if to clear it, then went on in his usual whisper. "He will be welcomed into the royal family, feted, celebrated, raised to a position of magnificence."

Marley gulped. He had no idea of Fiddleduster's aspirations, but he had no doubt that as soon as the prince heard the first notes of "The Hammering of the Slug," the fiddle player would be dismissed from the royal presence forever. And he himself, he reflected gloomily, would probably be thrown out of Cockenzie Rood for introducing him.

"Invitation!" The shadow was hissing again. "My master must be invited! There must be a written invitation, or he cannot cross the border!"

Albion, never the most perceptive, was looking at Marley with some curiosity. "Are you all right, Bill? You look a bit odd. And you keep talking to yourself. Can hear you muttering."

"No, no, Your Highness." Marley did his best to smile. "I'll make sure it's all arranged. Erm . . . he'll need an invitation from you, of course." He coughed. "Mr. Squint wouldn't dream of bothering you, splendid as you are, without a written invitation."

"Oh." Albion considered this. "Very proper. But you can tell your Mr. Squint it's OK. He can just pop up to the palace this afternoon, play a tune or two, and we'll all be hunky-dory. Easy-peasy. You tell him, and then you can be on your way."

Marley looked blank. Was he being thrown out of Cockenzie Rood already? "On my way where, Your Highness?"

The prince frowned. "Dear me, Bill. Thought spies were clever chaps. You're going to the House of the Ancient Crones, of course!"

The shadow was pressing hard against Marley's throat. He coughed again. "But, Your Highness —"

"Not another word!" Albion stamped his foot. "Are you my spy, or aren't you?"

The unhappy Marley nodded.

"Well, then! Off you go! Quick smart! And make sure the musician — what's his name again? Squiddle? — is here by three. Otherwise I'll do without him." And the prince turned to stomp off. As he turned, his foot struck the iron ladle left there by Marley the day before. "What's this? A ladle? Tidy it up, Bill. Now, this minute! Can't have rubbish lying around. Certainly not!"

The pressure on Marley's throat was agonizing. He was also beginning to feel angry. Albion might be a prince, but he was, when all was said and done, only a boy. What right did he have to be so overbearing?

"Just a minute," Marley began, and his tone was not conciliatory.

Albion swung around. "What is it now?" he asked crossly, his expression that of a fractious baby.

Marley opened his mouth to resign his position, to refuse to be a spy a moment longer, to say he was going home to bed and was going to stay there for a week—but he was forestalled. The shadow suddenly loosened its hold, and Marley blinked. Could he really see Fiddleduster Squint? A strange, translucent, shimmering Fiddleduster, with a furious expression on his cadaverous face?

I'm hallucinating! Marley thought. As he rubbed his eyes, the apparition seized the iron ladle, grunted, and hit Prince Albion fairly and squarely on the back of his head. Then it was gone. As the prince collapsed, Fiddleduster's shadow danced around him, waving its arms in glee.

"What's he done?" Marley was appalled. "He'll be thrown into the dungeons! He'll be there for life!"

The shadow quivered in front of him. "Not my master, Mr. Bagsmith. Not Fiddleduster Squint. Why, he wasn't even here! I called on his strength to help me, called on my master to lend me the power of his muscle and bone. And think about it, Mr. Bagsmith, think about it. Whose fingerprints will they find on that ladle? Why, yours! Yours, of course. Who was alone with the prince when he was hit? Why, you! You, and you alone!"

Marley went very pale. "But it wasn't me," he began. "It was you—"

"Me? You think you can say it was me?" the shadow mocked. "And who can catch a shadow? Nobody. So take him to the Howling Arms before anybody sees the terrible deed that you have done."

"But what . . . where . . . what will he do there?" Marley was finding it difficult to speak.

The shadow looked at him as if he was deranged. "He'll hear my master play. Then all will be well. Now, hurry! Hurry!" It circled Marley as if to encourage him. In doing so, it came closer to the shed, and for a moment the anxiously watching Gracie thought the shadow had seen her, as it made a sudden sharp zigzag away. It made no comment, however. Instead it continued to urge Marley to hurry, and she breathed a silent sigh of relief.

"Phew! I thought that horrible thing had spotted me," she whispered.

Marlon made a faint noise of disagreement. "Knows you're here, kid," he said. "At least, it felt something. Blast of Trueheart, maybe. Better get out sharpish."

Gracie was watching Marley manhandle the comatose form of Prince Albion into a wheelbarrow. He then looked around, evidently wondering how best to hide the prince, but instead of searching in the shed, he settled for his own coat and a selection of cabbages. A moment later he was wheeling the barrow away in as nonchalant a fashion as he could manage.

"Okey-dokey, kiddo," Marlon said. "Now's your chance to make a run for it!"

"Make a run for it?" Gracie was pulling on a pair of mismatched rubber boots from a pile heaped in a corner. "Make a run for it?" She sounded astonished. "I can't do that. I've got to follow them and make sure Albion's all right. That shadowy thing is evil. Really evil." She shivered. "I can feel it."

"Told you, kiddo. You felt it, and it felt you." Marlon flew a swift circle. "Sure you want to follow it?" He saw Gracie's face and chuckled. "That's my girl. Trueheart through and through. I'd better be offski—"

"Off?" Gracie was startled. "Off where?"

"Fetch young Marcus. See you, kiddo . . ." And Marlon looped out of the window and was gone.

Gracie looked after him. She was conscious of a feeling of relief, but butterflies had suddenly appeared in her stomach. "Don't be stupid, Gracie Gillypot," she told herself. "Marcus loves adventures, and it doesn't matter a bit what he thinks about me. Marlon's quite right. I need him. I can't cope with Prince Albion on my own . . ."

Auntie Vera fluttered down beside her. "Don't you worry, dearie," she said. "I'll come with you. I may be an ancient old bat, but I can take a message if you need me to. And that nephew of mine'll be back with your young man in no time at all."

"He's not . . ." Gracie began, and then stopped. Was Marcus her young man? She stood up and took a long deep breath. "It doesn't matter," she decided. "It doesn't matter at all right now. What matters is finding out what's happening to poor Albion!" And she opened the shed door and stepped outside.

Chapter Fourteen

The earth was shaking. Rocks and stones tumbled in all directions, and rabbits skittered for the safety of their holes. Trees rocked and lurched, and bushes were uprooted and flung to one side as if they were nothing more than wastepaper.

"OUT," rumbled a voice. "OUT. MEGGYMOULD, ARE YOU THERE?"

"ON MY WAY." The answer was somewhat muffled, and a flurry of dead leaves was flung high into the sky. "LEAVES IN MY MOWF. HOOOF! THERE. DAT'S CLEARED DEM." There was another land-slide from the far side of the hollow, and a giant slowly emerged wiping his mouth. Slowly and creakily, he pulled himself up to his full height, stretched his arms, and gave a wheezy groan. "STIFF, I AM. DE OLD BONES IS ACHING. HOW IS YOU?"

A second giant was rolling himself out from under a counterpane of green turf studded with astonished daisies. "I IS GOOD. OOOF! SUN IS VERY BRIGHT! WHERE LOVELY TRUNKLY?"

"I HERE TOO," said a third voice, and the last hillock fell into a scumble of loose stones as a giantess sat up. "HAPPY HUNDREDS, GREATOVER. HAPPY HUNDREDS, MEGGYMOULD. IS I AS PRETTY AS WHEN I WENT TO SLEEPY-BYES?"

"YOU IS MORE PRETTIER THAN EVER," Greatover told her. "UMPH! HAVE A RUMBLY IN MY TUMBLY!"

"ME TOO," Meggymould agreed. He looked around, rubbing the soil off his enormous arms. "WHAT DINNER SHALL HAVE?"

Trunkly was helping Greatover extract a gorse bush from his beard. "EGGSIES!" she said. "TRUNKLY WANTS EGGSIES FOR HER DINNER!"

Meggymould took a couple of tentative steps first one way, then the other. "MY FEETS IS PINS AND NEEDLING."

"YOU NEEDS DANCING," Trunkly told him. "LIKE THIS!" She flung out her arms and stamped around in a circle.

The rabbits shook in their burrows, and thousands of

birds flew up from the trembling trees of the forest. The waters of a nearby pond swirled and splashed, and far away in the House of the Ancient Crones, Val clutched at her teacup as it rattled in its saucer. "Whatever's happening?" she gasped. "Is it an earthquake?"

The Ancient One watched her plate quiver in front of her. "Possibly. But I think it's much more likely that the giants are awake. Trunkly's still young, and she likes to dance. Better make sure the china's stacked properly for the next few weeks."

Even as she spoke, a large jug jiggled its way to the edge of a shelf, hesitated, then crashed to the floor.

"Bother," Edna said. "I was fond of that jug. It belonged to my mother. Oh, well. Better sweep it up. Have you finished your breakfast, Val?"

Val was still staring at the tidal waves in her cup of tea. "How far away are they?" She sounded nervous. "The giants, I mean?"

Edna laughed. "At least ten miles. Maybe farther. I don't know exactly where they settled for their last hibernation."

"And how long will they dance for?"

"Not long. They're too big. Just walking wears them out. That's why they spend so much time asleep." Edna picked up a broom and began sweeping away the broken bits of china. "It's sad, really. There used to be hundreds of giants, and they were never any trouble. They just wandered about, then slept, then wandered again. But with the coming of the Five Kingdoms, their traditional paths were interrupted, and they lost heart. They're the simplest of creatures, you know. They can't understand why the people of the Five Kingdoms don't welcome them and love them, but they've gradually accepted that they must stay away."

Val looked scandalized. "But they'd destroy the kingdoms if they came anywhere near! Look at your jug! All the buildings would collapse!" She glanced up at the ceiling, where the spiders were rapidly reinforcing their webs. "And what about our house? We're ever so much nearer!"

The Ancient One put down her broom. "Haven't you ever wondered why the house moves about such a lot? Why the doors are always sliding up and down the corridor, and the mailbox is sometimes on the roof? It's so we can withstand any amount of Trunkly's dancing."

"Oh." Val did not sound particularly reassured, but as the tea in her cup had now calmed, she finished it quickly. "How many of them are there?"

"Only three." Edna's voice was sad. "Meggymould,

Trunkly, and Greatover. And when they go, there'll be no more. They'll be mountained, like all the old ones."

Val stared. "What do you mean?"

"The bigger they grow, the slower they get," Edna explained. "And eventually they get so enormous, they can't move at all. So they go to sleep, as usual, but instead of waking up every hundred years, they go on sleeping . . . and eventually they turn into hills or even mountains." She pulled a hankie out of her pocket and wiped her eye. "Umbleton didn't wake up last time, and he was a good friend of mine. We used to talk about the old days — the days before the Five Kingdoms. There aren't many of us left who remember."

"Hmm." Val remained unconvinced. "Well, as long as they don't decide to go thumping about too near here, I suppose it's all right. How long until they go back to sleep again?"

Edna began tidying up the breakfast things. "It depends. Maybe a week, maybe a month. They need to eat, and they need to find another comfortable resting place." She saw the expression on the Youngest's face. "It's nothing to be frightened of, Val. They eat leaves and birds' eggs and berries, not humans. And they'll probably wander even farther away this time."

"If you say so." Val got up from the table and yawned. "I'd better go back to the looms. Only three more cloaks to go, thank heavens. Although one of the finished ones does look as if someone's been eating toast all over it."

"That'll be Foyce," Edna said. "I'll have a look at it. Did Alf go off all right this morning?"

Val nodded. "Bright as a button. Dying to see Gracie again." She gave a sentimental sigh. "They do love our Gracie, those bats."

"Hardly surprising," the Ancient One said. "Now, we'd better get busy. Elsie's been working at the web for hours. She'll be needing her breakfast. And so will her chickens." She led the way to room seventeen. "Here we are, Elsie! I've left the kettle on for you. How's the web looking?"

Elsie slid off her stool and stretched. "Much as before," she reported. "Rather more lumps and bumps, perhaps, but they're a long way off. Nothing suspicious, I'd say. Oh, and Foyce isn't up yet. Do you want me to call her?"

The Ancient One shook her head. "Let her sleep a little longer. She's been doing better recently. We'll make a crone of her yet."

Val snorted. "Hmm. She's always picking on Gracie."

"Of course she does," Edna said calmly. "She's got years and years of unpleasantness and wickedness to be undone, and she's hardly been here five minutes. Look how long it took you, Val dear."

Val sat herself down at the loom without another word. Her previous life as thief, liar, and all-around criminal was not something she liked to be reminded of. She picked up the shuttle loaded with red wool and got on with her weaving.

Chapter Fifteen

Breakfast in the Royal Palace of Gorebreath had not been a happy meal. King Frank had glowered at Marcus from behind his newspaper, and Queen Mildred's attempts to broker some kind of truce had fallen on deaf ears. She had now taken the king away to get ready for a visit to Dreghorn, leaving Prince Arioso to try and cheer Marcus up.

"Come on," he cajoled. "Come and visit Nina-Rose with me." He blushed. "She's pretty enough to make any chap feel better. And her sisters will be there too. It'll be splendid fun! I know Father's looking a bit glum, but he'd be delighted if you came with us." He gave his twin brother a sideways look. "Father really likes Marigold, you know."

"Marigold?" Marcus was appalled. "But she's GHASTLY! She hasn't got a brain in her head! Besides, isn't she best friends with Vincent? They're about as daft as each other." He pulled irritably at a button on his jacket, and it fell on the floor. "And what do you mean—Father would be delighted?"

Arry picked up the button and tidied it neatly into Marcus's pocket. "Well . . ." He hesitated. "I think he thinks it might be rather nice if . . . I mean, there's me and Nina-Rose. We're practically engaged. Wouldn't it be fun if you and Marigold got together as well?" Arry gazed into space, a fatuous smile spreading across his handsome-but-somewhat-vacant face. "I say! Maybe we could even have a double wedding one day . . ."

"WHAT?" Marcus sprang to his feet. "Marry Marigold? I'd rather marry a . . . a . . . a bluebottle! It'd have more sense, that's for sure. Besides, what about Gracie? I like her a million trillion times better than any other girl I know. If I have to marry any-one, I'll marry her." He stopped, surprised at his own words. Did he mean what he had said? He found that he did. In fact, he was pleased that he did.

His brother picked up a spoon and put it down again. "I'm sure Gracie Gillypot's a splendid girl, but . . ." He did his best to be tactful. "But do you think she'd fit in with darling Nina-Rose? And Mother and Father? Isn't she a bit . . . different?"

Marcus scowled. "Yes," he said. "She is different. That's exactly why I like her. Honestly, bro, surely you know by now how much I hate all this royal puffing and huffing and speechifying."

Arry looked at Marcus, trying to understand his frustration. He was not a clever young man, but he was genuinely fond of his twin. At last, with a most unusual flash of intuition, he said, "You know what? I know why you like Gracie! It's because you're different too." He nodded, pleased with himself. "I'm right, aren't I?"

"Phew." Marcus smiled for the first time that morning. "Well done, bro. Yes. You're right . . . but what do I do about it? Nobody ever listens to me or takes any notice of what I want. Father's mad at me for ruining your day yesterday, and I'm really sorry about that, but it just shows the sort of guy I am. Useless at being royal. And now I'm stuck here when I really want to go and get Glee from the House of the Ancient Crones, and I ought to see Gracie to . . . to sort out a few things." He paused and rubbed at his already-untidy hair. "I think she might be a bit fed up with me, actually."

Arry, who suffered regularly at the hands of the highly demanding Nina-Rose, looked wise. "Girls are like that, you know. Tell you what! Take her some flowers. Works like a charm." A recent confrontation with his beloved floated into his mind. "Of course, diamonds work best of all. Why don't you take her a pretty bracelet? Or a brooch?"

"Gracie would hate diamonds." Marcus stalked across to the window and stared out in the manner of a prisoner peering through his bars. "Besides, how can I take her anything? Father said that if I didn't stay around for at least a week, I'd—" He swallowed. "I'd be the biggest disappointment of his life."

"Ah." Arry shook his head. "See what you mean. Difficult . . ." His brother's distress was troubling him, and he searched his mind for a solution. "Hey! What about Bluebell?"

"What about her?" Marcus asked, puzzled. Bluebell, Queen of Wadingburn, was a formidable woman. She strode around the Five Kingdoms offering advice to all and sundry, whether they had requested it or not. More usually it was not, but that had never been known to deflect her from her purpose.

"Get her to talk to Father." Arioso beamed, certain that he had solved the problem. "She likes you. You may think I don't notice things, but I do, you know. Bluebell likes you. Actually, she likes Gracie too. In

fact, I think she likes her better than— What's that noise?"

The brothers listened. There was a muffled squeaking coming from the chimney. A moment later a cloud of coal dust and a scatter of stones fell into the empty hearth, followed by a small and soot-encrusted bat.

"Oops!" it said.

Marcus grinned. "Hello, Alf. I had a feeling you'd turn up sometime."

"Mr. Prince!" Alf was unabashed by his unceremonious arrival. "Have you seen Miss Gracie? Is she here?"

Before Marcus could ask Alf to explain, there was a tapping on the window.

"Gosh!" Arioso's eyes opened wide. "There's another one! And it's bigger!" Aware of Marcus's unorthodox collection of friends, he turned to his brother. "Is this something to do with you?"

Marcus grinned and opened the window. "Marlon, meet my brother, Arioso. Arry, this is Marlon. And the grubby one is Alf. Alf, whatever were you—?"

"No time for that, kiddo." Marlon had flown to the prince's shoulder. "Urgent message. Ahem."

"Oh!" Understanding flooded into Marcus's mind. "Erm . . . Arry, why don't you go and get ready? I'll be with you in two ticks—I'll just find out what's going on in the world of bats." He hoped he was sounding sufficiently casual, but Arry hesitated in the doorway.

"Is everything all right?"

"Absolutely!" Marcus gave his twin a cheery wave, and Arioso obediently left the room, only to put his head back around the door a second later. "Are you sure there's nothing wrong?"

"No, no. Well . . ." Marcus was touched by Arry's concern. "If there is, I'll come and tell you. Promise."

As soon as Arioso had closed the door behind him, Marlon flew down to Marcus's shoulder. "Got a message from the kid. Says she needs you—needs you right now."

Marcus's heart began to hammer in his chest. "What's happened to her?"

"Not her." Marlon dropped his voice. "Prince Albion. Bopped on the head and carted off in a wheelbarrow."

Relief that Gracie wasn't hurt made Marcus hoot with laughter. "Poor old Albion! He can't like that much. But I bet he was asking for it. I've often wanted to bop him on the head myself. But . . . hang on a moment. I thought Gracie was back at home?"

"Spent the night in a shed." Marlon, having heard

Gracie's account of the events of the previous evening, was strongly of the opinion that Marcus could have done more to make sure she was safe. "Soaking wet. Came back to rescue you from the guardhouse. Bare feet 'n' all."

"WHAT?" Marcus looked so shocked that Marlon felt a pang.

"Maybe you didn't know, kid," he conceded. "But that's where she was. In a shed. And that's where we saw what happened."

Marcus was now striding up and down the room in agitation. "But that soldier—he said the path had come for her! I asked him twice! I'd never, ever have gone home if I'd had any idea Gracie was still around. Never! You know I wouldn't!"

Alf, hanging from the candelabra and doing his best to scrape away several layers of soot from his fur, nodded. "True love," he murmured. "True love."

Marlon flew in front of Marcus, flapping his wings to catch his attention. "Sorry, kid. But she could be in trouble. Albion's been wheeled off, and she's following him—"

"Right!" Marcus headed for the door, then slapped his head. "Oh, NO! Glee's not here! What shall I . . . I know. I'll take Arry's pony. Arry won't mind." He hurled himself out of the room and two minutes later was running across the stable yard. There was no sign of the stable boy, but Marcus had no time to waste. He saddled and bridled his brother's pony as fast as he could and clattered out of the yard, Marlon flying above him.

"Take it steady, kiddo," the bat warned. "Broken necks don't help nobody."

Marcus made no attempt to slow his speed. "Tell Gracie I'm coming," he said. "Tell her I'll be there as soon as I can. HURRY, Marlon!"

"Wilco." Marlon felt he had done his best. A moment later he was a speck in the distance.

Arioso, glancing out his bedroom window to check if it was sunny enough to wear his new pale blue satin coat, was just in time to see his brother galloping down the driveway. A second glance revealed that Marcus was riding Hinny, Arry's pony.

Arry sighed. "I knew something was up. Oh, dear. He's going to be in terrible trouble. Whatever will Father say?"

So disturbed that he failed to notice his buttons were done up the wrong way, Arioso hurried down the stairs and back to the dining room. "Bat?" he called. "Bat? Are you there?"

It had taken Alf longer to free himself from the coal dust and soot than he had expected, and he was still hanging from the candelabra cleaning his furry stomach. He looked at the anxious Arioso with interest. "Morning, Mr. Prince," he said. Then, feeling this wasn't quite right, he added, "I mean, good morning, Mr. Prince who's Mr. Prince's brother. I mean the Mr. Prince who's Miss Gracie's Mr. Prince, that is, Mr. Prince."

Arry, already suffering from stress, clutched at his head. "Erm," he said. "Erm . . ."

Alf flew down to perch on the enormous silver centerpiece. A small flurry of soot came with him. "Are you in love, Mr. Prince?" he inquired. "'Cause Miss Gracie and Mr. Prince—that's not you, Mr. Prince, but the other Mr. Prince—they are, but they don't know it." Alf sighed a romantic sigh and fanned himself with a wing. "I don't suppose you could help?"

Arry shook his head. "Erm . . ." He did his best to gather his thoughts. "Look here, Bat. I need to know. Is my brother in danger?"

Alf was delighted by the question. "He's gone to rescue his own true love," he said in his most dramatic squeak. "Did you see my uncle Marlon? He's a messenger. Ever so important, he is." Family pride got the better of Alf's sense of caution. "He knows everything, Unc does. He came flying from miles and miles away to warn Mr. Prince that Miss Gracie was in terrible danger. Her and the other Mr. Prince—Mr. Prince who's the prince at Cockenzie Rood. Bopped on the head and carried away in a wheelbarrow—"

"But . . ." Arry shut his eyes while he tried to process this alarming news. "You mean . . . You mean Prince Albion? He's been bopped on the head? Or was Gracie Gillypot bopped? I don't understand. And was Albion put in a wheelbarrow? How terribly undignified. How simply, utterly dreadful—"

Alf realized he had said too much, but it was too late. Arioso was on his feet, and before Alf could say another word, he was ringing a bell as loudly as he could. As servants came running, he hurried into the hallway. "Call the guard!" he ordered. "Where's Father? Where's Mother? We've got to call out the army, and we've got to do it at once!"

King Frank and Queen Mildred, hearing the furor, came hurrying down the staircase.

"What is it?" the king asked. "What's going on?"

Arioso wrung his hands. "Terrible news, Father.

Someone in Cockenzie Rood has kidnapped Albion and put him in a wheelbarrow, and Marcus has dashed off to rescue him!"

"No, he hasn't! He's gone to rescue Miss Gracie!" Alf squeaked indignantly, but nobody heard him. Offended, he flew up to a dark corner to make sure his wings were functioning properly before he set off after Marcus and Marlon.

King Frank frowned. "Are you sure of this, Arioso? Are you sure it isn't yet another of your brother's silly pranks?"

Queen Mildred put a hand on her husband's arm. "Of course it isn't, dear." She turned to Arry. "Did they send a messenger from Cockenzie Rood? Is he still here? Poor, dear Hortense . . . she must be so worried."

There was a sudden thump as Arry sat down and swallowed hard. There had indeed been a messenger, but the messenger had been a bat. And although Marcus dealt happily in the world of talking bats, Arry was certain his father and mother would not. In fact, now that he came to think about it, they would most probably think he, too, was indulging in a . . . What had his father called it? A silly prank. But he had to help Marcus . . .

"Erm . . ." Arry said. "The messenger had to leave. At once."

Queen Mildred gave him a puzzled look. "And he didn't want to speak to your father?"

Arry was floundering. He had never been good at telling lies, or even half-truths. He looked around for inspiration but found none. "He only wanted to speak to Marcus," he said lamely, then added, "He didn't want to speak to me."

"Hmm. Just as I thought." King Frank nodded. "It's some mischief or other. Didn't Marcus go to see Albion yesterday evening? This is some plot they've hatched up so Marcus can go off gallivanting again."

"Dearest, we don't know that," the queen said. "And what if Arry's right, and Albion has been kidnapped? Wouldn't it be too, too dreadful if we ignored a cry for help?"

The king hesitated. There was a small part of him, usually firmly suppressed, that admired Marcus's enthusiasm for adventures. This same small part, given space to express itself, also wished that Arioso was sometimes a little less cautious and obliging. "Ahem," he said. "You're sure you couldn't have misunderstood the message, Arry?"

Arry shook his head.

The king made up his mind. "Then you must take four of the guard and ride to Cockenzie Rood right now this minute. Take a messenger pigeon, and if Albion really has been kidnapped, you can send it to me . . . although I still have my doubts. And don't forget to assure King Dowby and the duchess that we will do all we can to assist them."

"That's right," Queen Mildred agreed. "And remember to send the pigeon to Dreghorn, dear. Your father and I will be there all day. Queen Kesta wants to plan a surprise party for Bluebell's birthday, although I'm not sure Bluebell will like it. Oh! Will Kesta have heard about poor Albion?"

The king sighed. "If she has, we'll know all about it the second we arrive. But let's be careful. If they haven't heard anything, we won't mention it. We don't want those girls weeping and crying and having hysterics if there's no need for it. Plenty of time for that once we've heard from Arioso."

Arry opened and closed his mouth. "But . . ." he began, as a new consequence floated into his mind. "But what about Nina-Rose? She'll be expecting me, and she'll be ever so cross if I don't come when I said I was going to."

"Nonsense." King Frank looked at his oldest son with

unusual disapproval. "This might be an emergency, and in the case of an emergency, we royals must always do what needs to be done!" He puffed out his chest as if it was covered with rows of shining medals awarded for Bravery in Action. "One day you'll be king, my boy, and then you'll have to take responsibility. Be a leader of your people! Best to get some practice now." He swung around to the servants lining the wall. "Prince Arioso will be riding out. Prepare his horse!"

"But, Father," Arry said quickly, "Marcus has taken my pony!" He hated riding, and he had watched Marcus ride away on Hinny, the only pony he had ever managed to stay on for more than fifteen minutes. "Besides, if I'm taking a messenger pigeon, wouldn't I be better going in a coach?"

Mildred, who knew exactly how her oldest son felt about riding, clapped her hands. "SUCH a good idea," she said. "But your father and I will be taking the coach to Dreghorn. Why don't you take my open carriage? I'll send some fruit and flowers for dear Hortense. And don't worry about darling Nina-Rose. We'll tell her you've been called away on an urgent mission of enormous importance, and she'll be so proud of you, Arry dear." And she bustled away to get things ready.

Arry went slowly upstairs to change his blue satin coat for something more serviceable. He was not looking forward to his mission. *What if this kidnapper chappie's out to collect a whole load of princes?* he thought. *Oh, bother it all. Things like this shouldn't happen in the Five Kingdoms. All I want is a nice peaceful life . . .*

A small dark shape flittered into view. "Hey, Mr. Prince who isn't Gracie's Mr. Prince! I'm off! Just came to say good-bye!"

"Oh," Arry said, with a distinct lack of enthusiasm. "I thought you'd already left. Where did you say you were going?"

"To find Miss Gracie and Mr. Prince, of course." Alf demonstrated his very best dip-and-dive technique, thereby drawing a heart in the air, an achievement that was totally lost on Arioso. "I'll tell them you're on the way if I get there first. Nice one, Mr. Prince!" And with a flip of his wings, he was out of sight, leaving Arioso feeling oddly comforted by the little bat's approval.

Chapter Sixteen

Fiddleduster Squint was lying back against the base of a broken statue. His home was a crumbling ruin on the edge of Howling Mere. Many hundreds of years before, it had been a fine baronial mansion, but time and wind and rain had reduced it to a heap of mossy stones, and the marsh had gradually seeped into the vaults and cellars, so a permanent chilly dampness haunted every room, whether there was a roof overhead or not. Gray, green, and evil-smelling spotted fungi sprouted in the corners of the walls, and rotting lengths of sodden velvet draped the cracked and discolored windows.

A movement at the entrance made Fiddleduster turn, and he saw his shadow slithering toward him. His expression darkened, and he raised a threatening arm. "How dare you take my power?" he hissed. "I felt it, as I always feel it! See how I am forced to rest, when I should be preparing for my glorious introduction to the Five Kingdoms!"

The shadow hung its head. "It was necessary, Master," it whispered. "It had to be done. One had no choice. But all will be well . . . all will be well."

"It will be so much the better for you if it is," Fiddleduster told him, with a cold glare. "Do I have the invitation? Did our dear, but very possibly unreliable, Mr. Bagsmith do as he promised?"

The shadow shifted from side to side. "Listen, Master. There is no written invitation, but the prince has asked to hear you play . . . and he has asked to hear you today. This very day!"

Fiddleduster pulled himself to his feet with an effort. "Where? Where is this to be? Without the written word, it will be impossible for me to cross the border!"

"If you cannot go to the prince, Master," the shadow said, and there was satisfaction in its voice, "then the prince must come to you. And so"—it gave a triumphant chuckle—"it has been arranged! At this very moment, Mr. Bagsmith is wheeling him to the Howling Arms to hear your angelic music."

"Wheeling?" Fiddleduster Squint asked. "The prince comes in a coach?"

"There was . . ." The shadow hesitated. "There was some persuasion necessary. That is why one was forced to steal your power, Master." It wriggled apologetically. "It was just a single blow, after all. One blow to ensure your future. Surely you can forgive, when so much is at stake?"

There was a pause, then Fiddleduster nodded. "Well done," he said, and he rubbed his bony fingers together. "Well done, indeed, dear Shadow. I should not have doubted my shadow. Not for a moment! And now, now I must get ready for this most auspicious of occasions." He cracked his knuckles gleefully. "How long before our visitor sets foot in the Howling Arms?"

The shadow quivered while it made its calculations. Marley had found the wheelbarrow excessively heavy; Prince Albion could never have been described as a slim youth; and it had taken longer than expected to negotiate the winding paths in the palace grounds and reach the main highway. Progress was not helped by the deviations necessary to avoid being seen, nor by Marley's constant complaints. It was obvious to the shadow that, had it not been for his terror of the consequences, Marley would happily have left the insensible prince dumped at the side of the road; only the fear that was knotting his stomach and squeezing his heart kept him moving. The shadow had left him pushing the cumbersome wheelbarrow along the first stretch of the narrow rutted lane that ultimately led to the Howling Arms; he had been sweating profusely and swearing under his breath, but moving steadily toward his destination.

"They will be here by midday or a little after."

"And there is no doubt that they will come?" Fiddleduster stretched to his full height.

The shadow snickered. "No doubt at all. Mr. Bagsmith knows what he must do."

"Excellent!" His master nodded. "Excellent. But you must return to him, Shadow. Return, and see he does not slacken. And I will hasten to the Howling Arms to wait for your arrival. Oh, what a meeting this will be!"

Chapter Seventeen

Gubble had woken up. For a moment he was disoriented; the slats of the bench above him reminded him of bars, and he lay blinking up at them, wondering where he was. "Ug," he remarked, and then remembered. "Gubble find Gracie." Rolling out from under the bench, he sat up and looked around. Behind him was Cockenzie Rood. In front of him was Gorebreath. Beyond Gorebreath the river Gore marked the border of the Five Kingdoms, and on the other side, as the crow flew, lay the Rather Ordinary Woods. Gubble grunted. Once through the woods, he would still have to make his way through the Less Enchanted Forest to reach the House of the Ancient Crones.

"Is far," he said sadly. "Poor Gubble."

The rumble of wheels made him look along the road, and he saw a cloud of dust in the distance.

Only too aware that not all the inhabitants of the Five Kingdoms approved of trolls, he went back behind the bench until the travelers had gone past. As the dust gradually cleared, he saw there were four mounted soldiers escorting an open carriage; after his rough handling the day before, Gubble began to panic. "No soldiers! No prisons!" he said. "No prisons for Gubble!" In his agitation he ran across the road, tripped on the grassy bank, and fell into the ditch on the far side with a loud splash. The ditch was deep and full of muddy water; Gubble's sudden arrival sent a family of ducks flapping and squawking out of the ditch and into the path of the oncoming horses. The leading horse reared in fright and spun around to bump heavily into Arioso's carriage, sending carriage, horses, and occupant careering across the road. The ducks squawked, the horses neighed, the soldiers swore, and Arioso shouted, "Kidnappers! Kidnappers! They're doing it again!"

Gubble put his fingers in his ears and stayed where he was. It wasn't until the ducks returned, one by one, that the troll felt it would be safe to emerge. Cautiously he scrambled and squelched his way to road level and peered through a clump of dandelions. The soldiers had regrouped and were attempting to straighten a bent axle and a twisted wheel while Arry sat disconsolately on Lodmilla and Turret's bench. The upset had ruffled his normally immaculate hair, and his coat was torn and grubby.

Gubble squinched up his piggy little eyes and stared. "URK! Marcus!" With a grunt of delight, he scrambled to his feet and hurried toward the prince, his fear of soldiers forgotten. This was a face he knew and trusted. "Where Gracie?" he asked. "Marcus go find Gracie?"

Even at his best, Gubble was not an attractive sight to those who did not know him and love him. Now, smeared with mud and with water weed draped over his head and shoulders, he resembled a nightmarish monster rising from the depths of the earth. Arry let out a yell and dashed for the shelter of the carriage.

Three of the soldiers took one glance and joined him, but Sergeant Scraggs was made of sterner stuff. "Looks like a troll to me," he muttered. "Simple chaps, trolls." Fishing in his pocket for his grandfather's silver watch, he held it high in the air.

Gubble slowed, wondering what was going on.

The sergeant began to swing the watch to and fro on its chain. "We . . . do . . . no . . . harm!" he said,

mouthing each word as clearly as he could. "You . . . go . . . back . . . to . . . hole . . . in . . . ground."

Gubble stopped, puzzled. He stared at the sergeant, and then at the bench where the prince had been sitting. "Gubble find Gracie. Marcus? Marcus tell Gubble." There was a shake in his voice, and his shoulders drooped. "Please. Gubble sad."

Sergeant Scraggs had a sympathetic heart, and he recognized the signs of genuine grief. He put the watch back in his pocket, stood up straight, and saluted the part of the carriage that he guessed concealed Arioso. "No danger here, sir," he reported. "Poor little chap's upset. Seems to have confused Your Highness for your brother, if you'll excuse my mentioning it."

The soldiers, somewhat shamefaced, got back on their feet. Arry's head appeared over the side of the overturned carriage. "Excuse me, Gubble old chap. Didn't recognize you under all that weed and stuff . . . but I'm Arioso, don't you know. Not Marcus . . ."

Sergeant Scraggs saluted for the second time. "Do I gather that you know this troll, Your Highness?"

"Not exactly know him, sergeant. I've met him once or twice. But——" Arry sighed. "My brother does."

Gubble wiped his face with a grubby hand. The result was not an improvement. "Where Gracie?"

Prince Arioso was famed for his politeness. Mothers up and down the length and breadth of Gorebreath exhorted their children to "Say 'please' and 'thank you,' just like 'is 'ighness." He was not often called upon to be polite to an excessively grubby troll, but he did his best to rise to the occasion. "I'm very sorry for the confusion, old boy. Apologies. We're twins, you see. Me and Marcus. We look the same . . . well, more or less. But I'm Prince Arioso." Arry paused, half expecting Gubble to clap. Or cheer, as was usual when one of the inhabitants of Gorebreath met the heir to the throne. There was no response other than a blink, however, and he went on, "Prince Marcus has gone to find your friend Gracie. And I am on my way to find Prince Marcus."

"Ug." Gubble nodded, satisfied at last. He stomped closer and inspected the bent axle. "Peasy," he remarked, and straightened it. The wheel was even less of a problem, and once it was back in place, he lifted the carriage and set it the right way up. As he did so, he noticed Arry's messenger pigeon, reproachfully peering out of its upside-down basket. Without bothering to undo the leather strap, Gubble snapped the lid open and sent it flying free. "Bye-bye, birdie."

"Oh . . ." Arioso looked up in consternation at the

pigeon wheeling in the air above his head. "Oh, dear. That wasn't meant to happen, you know. That was a special bird. It's supposed to carry a message . . ."

"Birdies like flying," Gubble told him. "Not baskets." He bent down beside the carriage, inspecting the wheels and giving the axle a final check. All seemed good, and he gave the carriage a congratulatory pat that all but knocked it over a second time. "Prince go. Gubble come too. Find Marcus, find Gracie." And climbing onto the velvet-covered seat, Gubble sat himself down, a puddle of dirty water spreading on either side of his solid green body.

"Oh." Arioso looked hopefully at Sergeant Scraggs, but the sergeant was enjoying the situation and refused to catch his eye. The prince sighed for the second time and climbed up beside his unusual traveling companion.

"Go," Gubble said helpfully, and then again, "GO!" The horses bucked, neighed, and did as they were told, Arry hanging on to the reins with one hand and clutching at the door with the other. The soldiers, taken by surprise, were left to gather their wits and their horses and follow as best they could.

Chapter Eighteen

Following Marley and the wheelbarrow without being seen had not been easy. Gracie, aware that the shadow might well sense her presence if she came too close, was forced to keep her distance; she was very glad to have Auntie Vera flying above and reporting progress.

"They've gotten stuck in the mud . . . No, he's managed to pull the wheelbarrow out again. Oh, my word! The language! Close your ears, dearie. Not the sort of thing a nice young girl should hear, and you a Trueheart too . . . There they go again. Now they're out of the palace grounds . . . Well, I never! Why are they going that way? Oh, I see. Not so easy to see them now that they're under the trees . . . but here they come again. Ooh! There's a big bump! That tubby young prince nearly fell out of the wheelbarrow. Goodness me . . . dearie, I don't like to interfere, but there's a very nasty-looking shadow slithering around the Bagsmith person . . . makes my fur stand up on end, it does . . . and looking at the Bagsmith, I'd say he's as scared as anyone can be. Positively green, he's so frightened . . . Whoops! They're off the path and into the bushes . . . There's someone coming, but he hasn't seen them . . . and now they're back on the path. Ooh . . . the wheel's gotten stuck . . . No! It's free again. And here they come to the crossroads . . . If you ask me, dearie, they're heading for Howling Mere . . . Is he going to dump the prince in the water, do you think? Sink like a stone, he would. Well—here's a thing . . . that horrid shadow has slipped ahead of the wheelbarrow . . . Whoops! Off it goes . . . Do you want me to follow the shadow, dearie? The Bagsmith won't know. He'd not notice a herd of elephants treading on his heels by the look of him."

Gracie looked up at Auntie Vera. "Do you think you could?" she asked. "Maybe the shadow's going to meet someone. It must have an owner somewhere, mustn't it? I mean, you can't have a shadow on its own, although we must be very near the border of the Five Kingdoms, and weird things do happen on the other side."

"I'm sure you're right, dearie," Auntie Vera said.

"Oh! The Bagsmith's definitely trundling along the path that goes to the Howling Arms. I'll pop down there and see what's going on. You'll need to be careful there, dearie . . . It's not a nice place at all."

Gracie watched Auntie Vera disappear into the distance, then began to tiptoe toward Marley Bagsmith. She could hear him muttering and grumbling as he pushed the wheelbarrow over the rain-soaked ground, and by weaving her way in between the trees and bushes, she managed to get a look at Prince Albion. He was still half covered by Marley's old coat, but the vegetables had long since been jolted out of the wheelbarrow.

"Actually," Gracie told herself, and felt distinctly cheered by the thought, "if anyone wants to follow us, it'll be really easy. The wheelbarrow's left a track all the way, and they're bound to notice the carrots and cabbages." She crept a little closer. Albion was pale and his eyes were closed, but something about his expression made Gracie wonder if he was really unconscious or only pretending.

"If he woke up," she said to herself, "I could try and get him away. But he's much too heavy for me to carry. Oh, if only Gubble was here!"

"Dearie! You must go back. Go back right now this

minute!" It was Auntie Vera, looking agitated. "There are things in that place you do NOT want to see. I know you're a Trueheart, dearie, but there's a clutter of hideous zombies cheering on a near-skeleton with a fiddle, and the noise he's making is enough to make your teeth fall out."

She paused to see how Gracie took the news, but Gracie merely asked, "Is the shadow there?"

"It belongs to the skinny skeleton fellow," Auntie Vera said with a shiver. "Seems it can slide away when he tells it to. Now, off you run, dearie—"

Gracie stayed where she was. "I'm really sorry," she said. "I know you mean to be kind, but I can't run away. Not until I know what they're going to do with Prince Albion."

Auntie Vera sniffed. "There's no telling some folk," she said, rigid with disapproval. "Well, well. I expect you know best, being a Trueheart and all. But if I was you, I'd take something to stuff in my ears. Whatever that skeleton's playing, it makes yowling cats sound like a lullaby."

"Good idea," Gracie said. "Oh! Did you hear that?" She moved forward as quietly as she could, but Auntie Vera was ahead of her.

"Of course I heard it." The bat was still offended.

"I'm a bat, dear. Bats have excellent hearing. I'm surprised you haven't noticed, seeing as you're a friend of my nephew. But there we go. You're only human, even if you are a Trueheart. Wailing, that's what that noise is. But I can tell you that the prince is waking up. He's taking his time about it, though."

Gracie listened intently as she tiptoed in between the trees bordering the narrow lane. The wheelbarrow had developed a loud squeak, but as well as the squeak, she could hear a series of moans, gradually increasing in intensity.

"Dare I let Albion know I'm here?" Gracie asked herself. "Would he hear me if I whispered? But it might make him call out, and that would be dangerous." She glanced up at Auntie Vera. "Please," she mouthed, "please, how far is it now to the Howling Arms?"

The bat didn't answer. She was flying very high, and Gracie thought she hadn't heard the question. She was about to ask again when Auntie Vera dropped like a stone. Landing on Gracie's shoulder, she whispered, "Quickly! Into the bushes! Hide, dearie, hide!"

Such was the urgency in Auntie Vera's voice that Gracie did as she was told without hesitating. Only when she was crouched down among tall stalks of bracken did she whisper, "What is it? What happened?"

Auntie Vera was shaking. "That nasty shadow, dearie. It's sliding back this way. Don't let it see you. Like I told you — there's nastiness down there. Nastiness and terrible evil."

Gracie stayed very still while she tried to think what she should do. If she marched after Marley Bagsmith and boldly demanded that he give Albion up, would he take any notice of her? What about Albion himself? Would he be able to walk away? And what was going on in the Howling Arms that had scared Auntie Vera so much? Gracie pulled thoughtfully at the end of her braid. She had met zombies from time to time when she lived with her evil stepfather and stepsister Foyce in the village of Fracture and had never found them especially terrifying. In fact, had anyone given her the choice between living with a zombie or living with her stepfather, she would have chosen the zombie every time. "And Truehearts always make evil things worse," she reasoned, "so the zombies aren't exactly evil. Just horrid to look at. And mostly dead. And that's not their fault, poor things. But then again, I suppose there may be other kinds." She looked at the still-quivering bat. "Dear Auntie Vera, you've been so wonderful. Would you feel strong enough to have a look to see what's going on now?"

Auntie Vera nodded and rose up into the sunshine. At once there was a squeak of recognition, followed by frantic twittering—and to Gracie's enormous relief, Marlon came winging down to find her.

"Watch it, kiddo. Hear there's dirty work afoot!"

Gracie was shocked to discover that her first thought was to ask if Marlon had found Marcus. "Really, Gracie!" she scolded herself as she turned to greet the bat. "Hello, Marlon! Did you see Albion?"

"Moaning and groaning fit to bust," Marlon reported. "And well on his way to the Howling Arms. Best get after him—that shadow's hissing in Marley Bagsmith's ear, and they're off at a gallop!"

"Oh, no!" Gracie struggled to her feet. "Are they very far ahead?"

"Couple of hundred yards." Marlon put his head to one side. "Holy moly! What's that?"

Gracie's hearing was nowhere near as acute as Marlon's. Even though she listened as hard as she could, she heard nothing unusual.

Auntie Vera appeared in between the bracken fronds. "He's at it again. Screeching and scratching. She shouldn't go there, Marlon, Trueheart or no Trueheart. Leave it to that other prince. Didn't you say he'll be here any minute now?"

"Another prince?" Gracie did her best not to sound too eager. "Is Marcus coming?"

"Sorry, kid." Marlon waved an apologetic wing. "Thought I'd said. He'll be here soon. Riding like a maniac. No need for a map. Cabbages all the way!"

"Must we wait for him? Shouldn't we follow Marley and Albion?" Gracie asked. She stood up and emptied bits of bracken out of her boots. "It sounds as if something terrible's going to happen to Albion at the Howling Arms."

"Only one way to find out," Marlon said cheerfully. "Off we go . . . but keep low, kiddo."

Chapter Nineteen

The eggsies had proved to be a problem. Meggymould and Trunkly had shaken several trees, but the results, though dramatic from the point of view of the local wildlife, had produced no eggs. Greatover had gone in search of berries and had done better. He also had two pockets full of hazelnuts, and all three giants were sitting in the hollow cracking the nuts and munching on the berries.

"GOOD BERRIES," Trunkly said with her mouth full. "EGGSIES TOMORROW?"

Greatover shook his head. "NO EGGSIES. WRONG TIME. ALL NESTS ARE EMPTY."

Meggymould was drawing in the earth with a stick as he ate.

Trunkly peered over his shoulder. "WHAT IS DAT? IS BOXES?"

"IS LITTLE PEOPLE HOUSES IN FIVE KINGDOMS," Meggymould told her. "HAVE CHIMNEY POTTLES. AND PEEPHOLES. AND LITTLE PEOPLE GROW THINGS." He scratched his balding head. "LITTLE PEOPLE GROW CHICKEN BIRDS, AND CHICKEN BIRDS HAVE EGGSIES ALL YEAR-ROUND."

"OOH!" Trunkly clapped her hands. "WHERE ARE CHICKEN BIRDS?"

"NOT FOR US." Greatover frowned at Meggymould. "CHICKENS ARE FOR LITTLE PEOPLE."

Trunkly put her head to one side and smiled her sweetest smile. "BUT TRUNKLY IS LITTLE . . ."

Greatover handed her the last of the nuts. "TRUNKLY IS GIANT. LITTLE PEOPLE ARE LITTLE PEOPLE." He heaved an enormous sigh that sent leaves swirling up into the air. "MUST KEEP AWAY FROM DE KINGDOMS."

Trunkly began to pout. "ONLY SOME EGGSIES, TRUNKLY WANT. NOT LOTS. JUST SOME." She held her hands up in the air. "LIKE FINGERS. THEN NO MORE. TRUNKLY PROMISE!"

There was a gentle rumbling—a sign that Greatover was thinking. This took time, and Trunkly and Meggymould knew better than to interrupt. They finished the last of the berries and had time for a couple of games of Shuffle Cone before the rumbling finally faded away.

"WILL TOSS DE COIN," the old giant announced. "WILL TOSS. HEADS IS WALKIES TO DE KINGDOMS." He stopped and checked to see that Trunkly and Meggymould were paying attention. "ONLY EDGIES OF DE KINGDOMS, UNDERSTAND? JUST DE EDGIES! BUT TAILS IS WALKIES TO DE SOUTH. AWAY FROM DE KINGDOMS. FAR, FAR AWAY." He put his hand into his pocket while Trunkly and Meggymould watched, Trunkly breathless with excitement. Carefully, very carefully, Greatover pulled out a coin. In his huge hand it was tiny, but the Ancient One would have recognized it as an oversize gold medallion celebrating the birth of King Lammas of Cockenzie Rood, great-great-grandfather to Prince Albion. "ONE, TWO, THREE—FLIP!" Greatover intoned, and the coin spun up into the sunlight. Up and up it went, and then down, down, down into Greatover's waiting palm. Catching it neatly, he slapped it onto his wrist and held it covered.

"SURE DIS IS WHAT YOU WANTS?" he asked.

"YES, YES, YES!" Trunkly's eyes were shining.

"MEGGYMOULD WANTS TRUNKLY HAPPY," Meggymould said firmly. He squeezed her hand, and she twinkled back at him.

"YOU IS TRUNKLY'S BESTEST FRIEND."

Greatover uncovered the medallion and revealed the head of a singularly unattractive squalling baby. A shadow fell across the old giant's face as he stared at it.

Trunkly could wait no longer. "WHAT IS?" she begged. "TELL YOUR TRUNKLY!"

"IS HEADS."

"HEADS? OH! HOW HAPPY IS I!" And Trunkly seized Meggymould and began a wild dance of joy.

In the House of the Ancient Crones, the looms shook, and a crashing sound from WATER WINGS suggested that nobody had remembered to put away the china.

Fiddleduster Squint paused mid-note in the middle of "The Slithering Reel" and watched the clouds of dust swirling down from the trembling roof beams of the Howling Arms.

"Dear me," he murmured to himself. "One suspects the giants are awake."

Chapter Twenty

On a normal day, the duchess would have noticed Albion's absence almost immediately. As it was, however, she had other things on her mind. Coming down the stairs for breakfast, she noticed the hallway looked strangely bare. Further investigation revealed that King Dowby's vast collection of silver cups, bowls, and shields for horse racing, jumping, and dressage had disappeared. So, too, had a number of other silver items from the dining room and reception rooms. Of Bullstrop there was no sign, and when the duchess began to ask questions, it appeared that he had taken his leave of the kitchen staff the evening before, remarking that he'd had quite enough of the duchess's airs and graces, and was off the next day to stay with his great-aunt in Niven's Knowe. Or his uncle in Gorebreath. Or his old school chum in Dreghorn—unless, that was, he decided to settle down with his mother in Wadingburn.

"That is NOT a great deal of help," the duchess said to herself as the last of the kitchen maids departed. "Oh, dear! We've never had a burglary before. What are things coming to? It's just as well that Dowby's away. He'd make a terrible fuss and probably call out the army and upset everyone. Hopefully we'll find the thief before Dowby gets back. I'll go and see if anything else is missing and make a list." And, having equipped herself with a large piece of paper and a pen, she went to check the rest of the palace.

She was interrupted by a loud and imperious ringing at the front door, followed by a booming voice. "Hortense? Hortense! Where are you, my dear? You seem to have lost all your servants, so I've let myself in."

"Bluebell!" The duchess hurried to meet her friend, who was already striding down the hallway. "Bluebell! I'm so pleased to see you! We've had a horrid burglary, and I'm just checking to see what's gone."

Queen Bluebell of Wadingburn pulled out her lorgnette and surveyed the empty shelves with a distinct lack of sympathy. "Taken Dowby's trophies, I see. Good riddance, I'd say. Made the place look like a second-rate pawnshop. Still, I suppose burglary shouldn't be encouraged. Any idea who it might have been?"

"I don't think there's any doubt about it," Hortense said. "We had a new butler, but I told him last night that his services were no longer required, and he seems to have gone off with as much as he could carry."

Bluebell nodded. "Anyone see him go?"

"It must have been quite late last night, when we were all in bed." The duchess looked at her list of stolen goods. "But why would he want Dowby's silver cups? Surely he can't sell them. They've got Dowby's name all over them."

"Silver melts," Bluebell informed her, with a knowledgeable wink. "Better get them back fast, I'd say, or they'll be turned into coins of the realm, and you'll find yourself spending Dowby's challenge cups on peas and potatoes." She gave her friend an encouraging hug that left the duchess breathless. "Cheer up, old girl. I'll lend a hand. Always wanted to do a bit of sleuthing. Your Albion won't be any help, of course."

Hortense opened her mouth to defend her cousin, but honesty forced her to admit that Bluebell was right, and she said nothing. The queen threw herself into an armchair and went on, "Shame you haven't got little Gracie Gillypot here and young Marcus. Proper sense of adventure, those two. That's the kind of spirit I like to see."

The duchess looked up. "They were here last night, as it happens. Hmm. I wonder if Marcus noticed anything when he left?" A flush of embarrassment turned her cheeks pink. "Actually, that was why I sacked Bullstrop. He thought Marcus and Gracie weren't respectable and had Marcus shut in the guardhouse with Bobble, Gracie's pet troll."

"Gubble," Bluebell corrected. "And I wouldn't say he was anybody's pet. That troll has a mind of his own, even if it isn't a very big one." She gave a snort of amusement. "So what happened to Gracie? Did you lock her up too?"

"Albion said . . ." Hortense stopped. What *had* Albion said? He'd certainly told her that he'd ordered a coach for Marcus and the troll. That she remembered clearly. But what had he said about Gracie? That she'd gone home? Yes, she was sure that was it, and at the time she hadn't thought to question him further. "He said Gracie had gone home. But . . ." The duchess began to look worried. "Could she really? Is that possible? Where does she live, Bluebell?"

"House of the Ancient Crones. Miles away, outside the Five Kingdoms." Bluebell waved her lorgnette in

the air. "She couldn't have gone home. Something's going on. Good thing I popped over!"

"Yes." Hortense nodded. "And why did you come, Bluebell, dear? Not that it isn't the best thing that's happened today. I'm only too delighted you're here, but I wasn't expecting to see you until your birthday."

"That's what I wanted to talk to you about." The queen dropped her voice. "A little bird told me that Kesta's planning a surprise party. Such nonsense! I had a party when I was eighty, and I don't want another until I'm ninety. Can't be dealing with such things, so I'm relying on you to let Kesta know that, without her knowing I know. If you see what I mean."

Hortense did. "I'll do my best," she said. "I had a card saying she wanted to talk to me. And I happen to know she's asked Queen Mildred and King Frank over to Dreghorn for the day."

Bluebell gave a gusty sigh. "There you are. They'll be plotting cakes with enough candles to burn Wadingburn Palace to a cinder. But forget that. What are we going to do about this burglary of yours? Are there any clues? Have you looked outside?"

This idea had not occurred to the duchess. She put down her paper and pen. "Clues? Do you really think there might be some?"

"Could tell us which way he's gone." Bluebell heaved herself out of the armchair. "He took a lot of things, didn't he? So his bags must have been heavy. He might have stashed the loot somewhere nearby and be planning to fetch it later tonight."

Hortense looked at her companion in admiration. "*Stashed the loot?* Goodness, Bluebell! Anyone would think you're a regular detective. Come on. Let's go and see." And pausing only to pick up her shawl, she took Bluebell's arm, and the two of them sailed outside.

As they began to circle the palace, the duchess remarked, "I've just remembered something. Albion claimed someone was throwing carrots at him yesterday morning. I didn't think anything of it at the time, but supposing he was right? And Lubbidge—that's the gardener's boy—got himself locked in a shed in the vegetable garden, and he had a nasty bruise on his head when I saw him later."

Bluebell's eyes shone. "Excellent! Let's check the vegetable garden right now!"

The two old women marched around the corner of the palace . . .

. . . and stopped dead.

There, in the vegetable garden, right outside the garden shed, were the unmistakable tracks of a wheelbarrow.

Deep, heavy tracks — the marks of a wheelbarrow that was heavily laden. And the tracks led away from the palace, away from the garden.

Hortense looked at Bluebell, and Bluebell looked at Hortense.

"Do you know what I'm thinking, Hortense, old bean?" Bluebell asked. "I'm thinking it's not only Gracie Gillypot and that young man of hers who can have adventures. We may be old, but we're not past it yet. Let's track him down!"

"Absolutely!" The duchess swirled her shawl around her in the style of a bullfighter flinging on his cloak. "It's time we older ones took a stand. Oh! Shouldn't I tell Albion that we're going out? Not that he'll worry, of course. He wasn't even up when you arrived this morning, so he's probably still having his breakfast."

Bluebell frowned. "Just leave him to it. If he does worry, it'll do him good. I never tell Vincent where I'm going. Keeps the boy on his toes."

"Should we arm ourselves?" Hortense wondered. "If it was Bullstrop who did the burglary, he's a tall man. I'm sure the two of us will be more than a match for him, but it's best to be prepared. He might have . . ." She paused, searching for the right word.

"Partners in crime," Bluebell suggested. "Good

thinking." She opened the shed door and looked inside. "What about a pitchfork?"

Hortense considered the rows of agricultural implements. "I think I'd rather have a hoe." And then, "Look! An apron! Could it be Gracie's? And the sacks . . . It looks as if someone was sleeping here last night!" She clutched the apron to her ample bosom. "Oh, my goodness. Do you think that poor child was here all the time?"

"If she was, she might have seen your burglar." Bluebell sounded excited rather than upset. "And if I know Gracie, she'll have gone after him. Come on, Hortense! Choose your weapon, and we'll be off. Tally-ho, 'n' all that!"

Hortense, Dowager Duchess of Cockenzie Rood, waved her hoe. "Tallyho, indeed!"

Prince Albion was most certainly not worrying about his cousin. He was much too worried about himself. His head hurt, and he was bruised all over from the jolting and bumping he had suffered during the journey. He had no idea where he was, and he had no idea who was pushing him; he was facing forward, and all he could see through his glazed and aching eyes was a winding track that had an unpleasantly unkempt look about it.

"Stop!" he ordered, waving a limp arm. The wheelbarrow went faster. "Help!" he tried, but no help came. His head was still far too sore to try any kind of movement, and, even if that had not been the case, he was much too fearful for his own safety to make any attempt to jump out of the wheelbarrow. Albion shut his eyes, then opened them again, but the pain was still there.

I'm being kidnapped! was his next thought. *First they threw carrots, and now they've got me! Huh! This'll make Cousin Hortense sorry she didn't believe me. But where am I going?* He squinted ahead and saw a ramshackle roof half hidden among the trees—a roof that did not hold out much promise of comfort, warm baths, and chocolate cake. As they drew nearer and nearer, it became all too obvious that all that would be offered was extreme discomfort of the rough-hewn-boards-and-spiders variety.

And then the noise began.

Albion had never heard anything like it. It made his eyes water and his brain feel as if it had been stuffed with jangling shards of glass. He stuck his fingers in his ears, but it made no difference. "Owwwwww!" he wailed. "OWWWWWWWW! Tell it to stop!"

The noise stopped as suddenly as it had begun, and Albion breathed again. *Phew,* he thought, *that was terrible.*

Awful. Torture . . . that's it! Of course! They've brought me here to torture me. Torture me for money! He struggled to sit up but was defeated by his own weight. "If you want money," he said out loud, "you can have it! Whatever you want! Just say . . . my father's the king, don't you know." A terrible doubt as to what kind of value King Dowby would put on his only son seeded itself at the back of his mind, but Albion did his best to ignore it. "You! Whoever it is that's pushing this wheelbarrow! I'll make you a lord! A duke! An earl! I'll make you rich beyond your wildest—"

"Hush . . ." The voice that whispered in his ear chilled him to the back of his bones. Albion gulped and was silent.

"Hush, dear sir!" the voice went on. "My master waits for you within the humble walls of the Howling Arms. Pray excuse us for the rough-and-ready way in which we brought you to this poor place. Mr. Bagsmith, pray assist His Highness to his feet!"

It was only as Marley came around the side of the wheelbarrow to offer his arm that Albion realized who he was. He stared at Marley, his face turning a deep and furious purple. "YOU! It was YOU who kidnapped me? It was YOU who brought me to this horrible place? How . . . how DARE you! I TRUSTED you! You were my SPY! You're fired, Bill whatever-your-name-is. You're fired!"

Marley Bagsmith scowled. Had the shadow not been constantly hovering around his shoulders, he would have been sorely tempted to accept Albion's offers of fame and fortune, but he was much too much of a coward to take the risk. He half lifted, half pulled the prince out of the wheelbarrow and set him on his feet outside the front door of the Howling Arms. Albion began to protest, but as he caught sight of the sinuous shadow, its long arms holding Marley in a close embrace — or was it imprisonment? — he was silent once more.

The door to the Howling Arms opened, and Gruntle Marrowgrease stepped out. "Are you the fellow Mr. Squint's expecting?" he asked. "Because if you are, you'd better come in. He's been waiting for you, and the practicing ain't doing my trade any good. No good at all. So come on in, and let's get it over with. Not," he added hastily as he suddenly noticed the shadow wrapped around Marley Bagsmith, "not that Mr. Squint isn't one of my best customers. A fine fellow, to be sure. But there's a time and a place for the fiddle, and there are those who like it, and those who don't." And before Albion could say a word, the landlord picked him up and carried him into the darkness behind the door.

There were no windows in the Howling Arms, unless you counted the narrow slits high up under the roof beams. A few guttering candles provided all the light there was, and Albion, still groggy from the blow to his head, stared around in bewilderment. At first he could see nothing beyond the flickering flames, but gradually he realized that someone was speaking from the darkness on the other side of the room. Someone excessively tall and thin, with a face so like a skull that Albion shivered.

"Please be seated, Your Highness . . . please take your place. We welcome you. One is honored, truly honored by your presence . . . our noble prince. The prince of princes, dare one say."

Albion began to relax a little. Whoever this person was, they had the right attitude. He screwed up his eyes to see better; the speaker was shrouded by shadows and appeared to be standing behind a thick white line drawn across the floor.

"I can't see you properly," Albion said plaintively as he sat down on the hard wooden chair Gruntle Marrowgrease was offering and put his feet up on a nearby canvas bag. Still far from comfortable, he tried to pull the bag nearer but was defeated by its weight. "Who are you, anyway?"

"Fiddleduster Squint, at your service. The musician of your dreams; the instigator of music that will charm you for now and evermore."

There was a faint spatter of applause. Albion became aware of movement behind Fiddleduster but was unable to make out any individual shapes. "Oh," he said. "Oh. So are you the chap Bill was telling me about? Why didn't you come up to the palace?" He rubbed the bump on his head and stared reproachfully into the darkness. "Is this why he brought me here?"

"Pray excuse me, Your Highness. There was . . . there was a problem . . . a problem that could not be overcome." The voice was silken smooth. "And such a noble, such a generous prince as yourself will surely forgive the true artiste in his search for a patron."

"That's all very well," Albion said. "But you can't go around kidnapping princes, you know. It doesn't do. It doesn't do at all. I could get very cross about it, actually."

"Then we must keep you no longer than is necessary," Fiddleduster purred. "Prepare yourself, Your Highness. Prepare for true beauty." He took out his fiddle bow and poised it over the strings. "I will begin!"

Albion was frozen where he sat, incapable of movement or thought. The noise was even more excruciating

than it had been the first time he heard it; his eyes began to water and his nose to run, and he gasped for air like a dying fish.

"There, Your Highness!" Fiddleduster held his bow high as the last notes of "The Hammering of the Slug" died slowly away. "Is that not poetry? The quintessence of loveliness?"

Albion went on gasping. Fiddleduster smiled. "I see you are overcome. That is often the case when I play for the first time. One is honored. What shall I play now? 'The Smothering of Arduous Hardbone'?"

"NO!" Albion found his voice at last as he staggered to his feet. "No, no, NO! It's terrible! It's the most disgusting noise I ever heard in my entire life, and I never, never, NEVER want to hear it again!" He waved his arms and broke into hysterical laughter. "LOVELY? POETRY? It's like cats being murdered a million trillion billion times over . . . ha-ha-ha-ha-HA!" And he hurled himself out the door and into the sunlight. Shock and horror gave him wings, and he ran into the brightness and up the path as fast as his short, stout legs could carry him.

He left silence behind him.

A long, ominous silence.

Then Fiddleduster spoke, and his voice was pure

venom. "He laughed. That fat, foolish prince laughed at my music. For that he will suffer . . . and all Cockenzie Rood will suffer with him. Oh, how they will suffer! I shall bring chaos and destruction upon them all until the crying and screaming echoes the length and breadth of the Five Kingdoms!"

Gruntle Marrowgrease said nothing as Fiddleduster Squint opened the back door and made his way outside, closely followed by the shadow. As the door closed behind them, the bartender spat into a beer mug and began to polish it, a grim expression on his face. "That'll mean trouble. It doesn't do to upset the likes of him, Mr. Bagsmith. It doesn't, indeed. Heigh-ho! If it wasn't for the border line, that bumptious young fellow would have been mincemeat. Chewed and chawed to the marrow, I'd say." And he thumped the beer mug onto the bar by way of emphasis.

Marley, who was well accustomed to the internal gloom of the Howling Arms, shuddered. He had seen, as Albion had not, how Fiddleduster Squint had leaped forward when the prince laughed, his eyes glittering, and his bloodless lips drawn back into a snarl that showed his razor-sharp teeth. He had also seen how the invisible barrier had brought Fiddleduster to a shockingly sudden stop, exactly as if he had hit a wall of glass.

Marley felt in his pocket for a coin or two. He was profoundly grateful that he was on the Five Kingdoms' side of that invisible wall; relief was now telling him that a strong drink was necessary for a full recovery.

Gruntle, without being asked, poured half a pint of watery beer and handed it across the scratched and splintery bartop. "On the house," he said. "But when you've finished that, be on your way. I don't cater to princes. Nor them who bring them here, neither. Ruins my reputation."

One look at Gruntle's face was enough to convince Marley that argument would be futile. He downed his beer in a single swallow, dumped the mug back on the nearest table, and tried to take his leave. To his horror, he found that his legs appeared to have become disconnected from his brain. "Can't move," he said. "Can't move!"

A croak of laughter came from the darkest shadows beyond the line, where Mucus, Mildew, and Corruption were crouched.

"'Twas the power of the music," Mucus said.

"It twists the mind," Mildew agreed.

"And dulls the senses." Corruption gave a harsh cackle.

Gruntle Marrowgrease snorted. "Dulls the senses, does it? So it seems I'm stuck with you, Marley Bagsmith. Humph! If you can't move, you'd better polish these glasses. I don't have no freeloaders in my establishment." And he dumped a heap of mugs in front of Marley, together with a greasy rag.

As Marley slowly began his task, the landlord stepped away to open the wooden hatch leading to the cellar, where the beer casks were kept. "It's OK, Mr. Bullstrop," he said. "You can come out now." There was no response, and Gruntle raised his voice. "TAKE THE WOOL OUT OF YOUR EARS, MR. BULLSTROP! I said, you can come out now. What was it you was wanting to talk to me about? Something to do with silver?"

Chapter Twenty-one

The Ancient One stared at the fine silver fabric stretched in front of her on the web of power. A sharp, raised line was running from one side to the other as if a thread had been pulled. As she watched, the gleaming silver on the nearer side began to dim, slowly turning an ugly gray.

"Oh, dear," she said. "Elsie, have a look at this."

Elsie got up from the secondary loom. "Anything to get away from that dreadful scarlet," she said. "Still, we've only got a couple more cloaks, and then we'll be finished." She stretched. "It may be good money, but I'll be delighted to see the back of them. What's the matter?"

"Someone, or something, has tried to break across the border protecting the Five Kingdoms," Edna told her. "See how clear it is!"

"Can you tell where it happened?" Elsie asked.

Edna sighed. "If only I could. It's a vicious attack, though. Look at the color."

"But at least it's still outside the kingdoms," Elsie pointed out. She peered more closely at the web. "Is it my imagination, or are those lumps and bumps getting bigger?"

The Ancient One took another look. "You're right. The giants must have decided to come this way after all. Never mind. They aren't dangerous, and they know not to go too near the border. I'm far more concerned about this attack. We'll strengthen the enchantment . . . There's not much else we can do until we know more."

Val came wandering into room seventeen, yawning. "Foyce and I are having a cup of tea," she said. "Would either of you like one? And is there any news of Gracie?"

"Not yet." The Ancient One was loading her shuttle from a basket beneath her stool. "But I'm sure there'll be news quite soon."

Val's gaze sharpened. "Why are you using that silver filigree thread? Is there an emergency?"

"Not that I've heard." Edna's voice was very calm. "But someone tried to break across the border, so I'm making sure it hasn't been weakened." She tied in the thread and began to weave with long steady throws of the shuttle.

The filigree sparkled brightly against the gray, and Val folded her arms.

"Something's wrong. I know it is. I can tell, you know. I may be the youngest of you all, but I have feelings in my toe bones, and my toe bones are telling me that something's just not right."

"That's because Gracie's wearing your slippers," Elsie said tartly. "You've been grumpy ever since she left."

Val snorted. "I've been worried, if you don't mind. And Gracie's welcome to my slippers whenever she wants them. I just hope they've kept the poor girl's feet warm, wherever she's gotten to."

"Hush, girls," the Ancient One interrupted. "I can't concentrate with you two arguing. Elsie, those cloaks need to be finished as soon as possible. And, Val, we need to figure out who's going to deliver them if Gracie doesn't get back in time. You might have to take them, dear. But for the moment, perhaps you and Foyce can make sure the crockery's safe. If the giants are heading this way, we're in for some serious disturbance."

Chapter Twenty-two

Albion managed almost a hundred yards at a sprint
before his body noticed what was happening and put
in a formal complaint. His legs gave way, and with a
loud groan, he collapsed into the grassy strip beside
the path. "Oooooh!" he wailed. "Oooooh!"

Gracie, her ears still ringing from Fiddleduster's
music, came running toward him. "Prince Albion! Are
you all right?" She knelt beside him as he lay back and
closed his eyes with a dramatic moan. Gracie glanced
up at Auntie Vera, who was hovering over her head.
"Is Marcus anywhere near yet? Albion needs help!
What do you think they did to him?"

Albion's eyes stayed shut, but he managed a mar-
tyred smile. "Tortured . . ." he whispered. "I've been
tortured . . ."

"That's terrible!" Gracie said. "We must get you home at once— Oh! Where's Marley Bagsmith?"

Albion's smile faded. "He's a ruffian! A thug! He kidnapped me! ME! Prince Albion!" The prince's tone suggested that it would have been fine for Marley to kidnap anyone else, and Gracie's sympathetic expression wavered. "When I get home, I'll send out the guard. I'll have him thrown in the dungeons!" Albion was now sitting bolt upright, the better to shake his pudgy fists. "It won't do! I won't have it! I thought he was going to be my spy and find things out for me, and what does he do? First he bops me on the head, and then he kidnaps me! And all because he wants me to see some weirdo who plays the fiddle like a load of scalded cats!"

"But it wasn't actually Marley who hit you," Gracie began, but Albion was in no state to listen.

"Of course he did. I trusted him, and what's more I gave him loads of money, and he bopped me on the head, I tell you . . ."

As Albion continued to rant, Auntie Vera settled herself on a nearby bush to doze, and Gracie began to think of other things. She was getting less worried about the prince's state of health by the second; anyone who could talk so much and for so long must be reasonably all right. She did her best to look interested, but in the back of her head, she was considering the best way to transport him back to the palace. Would he get back in the wheelbarrow? It seemed unlikely.

Marlon, flying down to report, chuckled as he heard the prince's plaintive ramblings, but his news was sufficiently urgent to prevent him from taking time to listen for long. He had noticed Fiddleduster Squint's exit from the back of the Howling Arms and had been sufficiently interested by that strange gentleman's evidently apoplectic state of mind to follow him, keeping his ears wide open as he flew. What he heard made him fly a sudden, shocked zigzag.

"Holy moly!" he muttered, and it was only when Fiddleduster trailed under the broken archway of his ancient ruin that the bat circled slowly away. He was thinking hard. "A zombie on the warpath, swearing terrible revenge on the Five Kingdoms. Does he mean it? Could well be. And what have we got to stop him? The Trueheart, the prince, and me, Marlon Batster—"

"Don't forget me, Unc!" The squeak was right behind Marlon and made him swerve.

Alf twittered in delight. "You're losing it, Uncle M! You never heard me, did you? Alf—super-silent bat!"

More shaken than he would ever have admitted,

Marlon took refuge in being cross. "This ain't no time for the funnies! Where've you been?"

Alf giggled. "I met the other Mr. Prince who looks like our Mr. Prince, and he's on his way to find Miss Gracie and our Mr. Prince and the other one. The one in the wheelbarrow."

Marlon digested this news. He had no very high opinion of Arioso, but reinforcements might be necessary. "Okey-dokey. Now, pin back your ears. Gotta job for you. See that place below? Ruins 'n' all?" His nephew nodded. "Get down there. Watch. Listen. There's one angry zombie, and I want him checked. Every word he says. Every step he takes. Sharp, mind! There could be dark stuff brewing." He gave the little bat a searching look. "Get it?"

Alf's eyes shone, and he raised one wing in a salute. "Got it! Alf Batster never fails! See ya, Unc!"

As Alf fluttered down to the ruins of Howling Castle, Marlon had flown to find Gracie. Albion's tale of woe was continuing unabated, but as the bat circled toward them, there was a clattering of hooves from the opposite direction, and Marcus came galloping into view. Gracie jumped to her feet, her cheeks scarlet. With a shout of relief, Marcus slid off the saddle, rushed across the grass, and hugged her.

"Oi!" Albion struggled to his feet in indignation. "What's going on? Put that girl down! You're meant to be rescuing ME! Hey! MARCUS! I'm talking to you!"

Marcus, suddenly shy at having so obviously shown his feelings, let Gracie go. "Hello, Albion. Thought you'd been kidnapped?"

Albion pouted. "I have. I was. It was TERRIBLE!" He swayed to and fro while he tried to make up his mind if a faint would make Marcus realize how much he had suffered. As Marcus immediately turned back to Gracie, he decided against it. "Look here, Marcus old boy — it's not good enough! I've been bopped on the head! And then wheeled off to be tortured!"

"Sounds nasty," Marcus said in an offhand way. "But you look OK now."

"I most certainly am NOT!" Albion puffed out his cheeks. "I'm . . . I'm in shock!"

Gracie decided it was time to intervene. "I do think we should get him back to the palace. He still looks pale, and he was unconscious for a very long time."

"I was," Albion said proudly. "I was unconscious all the way down the vegetable garden and all along that horrible windy path. You've never seen so many ruts and bumps, Marcus, and I felt every single one of them. I'm feeling very poorly."

Marcus gave Gracie the faintest suspicion of a wink as he said, "You're quite right, Albion. You're a poor old thing. Look, why don't we put you on Hinny? She's the gentlest pony ever, and it won't take long to get you home— What's the matter?"

Albion was backing away, trembling. "No!" he said. "No! I can't! I can't ride! No ponies!"

"But—"

Marcus was about to argue, but Gracie saw that Albion was genuinely terrified. She stepped between the two princes. "It's OK," she said soothingly. "We'll think of something else. Maybe one of us could go and get help from the palace. They must be ever so worried about you." She turned to Marcus. "Did you stop in there on your way?"

Marcus stared at her as if she had lost her mind. "Of course not! Marlon said you might be in danger, so I came straight here!"

"Oh." Gracie smiled so happily that it made Marcus look down at his boots in pleased embarrassment. "Thank you! Erm . . . it would probably be quickest if you ride there while I look after Prince Albion."

There was a loud protesting wail. "No! You can't leave me! What if that creature comes to get me?"

Marcus folded his arms. "Come on, Albion. You want to get home, don't you?"

Albion nodded.

"Then there's only one answer. If you don't want to ride Hinny, and you don't want me to go and fetch help, it'll have to be the wheelbarrow." And before his fellow prince had time to protest, Marcus strode off toward the Howling Arms.

By the time he returned, Albion had grumpily agreed that there was no other option. Gracie did her best to make the wheelbarrow more comfortable with handfuls of bracken and Marcus's jacket, but the invalid still complained nonstop as they began their journey back toward the palace. It was an odd little procession. Marcus wheeled Albion, and Gracie followed behind leading Hinny. Marlon, keeping an ever-watchful eye out for Alf, circled above them. Of Auntie Vera there was no sign.

"I never thought I'd be so miserable," Albion wailed. "OUCH! That hurt! Can't you be more careful? OUCH! You might try and avoid the bumps! OUCH! The bracken's tickling my neck, and I'm sure it's giving me a horrid rash . . . OUCH! OUCH! OUCH!"

After rather more than an hour of this moaning, Marcus had had enough. He was hot, his back was aching, and his hands were getting blisters. "Albion," he warned through gritted teeth, "if you don't shut up, I'm going to dump you on the grass and leave you."

There was an even louder wail. "But you don't understand! I'm suffering! It's all very well for you, Marcus. You're beefy and strong, but I'm a flower compared to you. A fragile flower! Even my cousin says I'm sensitive, and I am, you know, I'm ever so sensitive and I— Oh, oh, OH, OUCH!"

Marcus, irritated to the point where he could hardly speak, had turned a corner too fast and run into a substantial rock. The wheel twisted, the barrow tipped, and Albion found himself lying on the grass staring up at the sky. He was so outraged at what he was quite certain was a deliberate upset that he completely failed to notice the small bat zooming across his vision.

"Miss Gracie! Mr. Prince! Uncle Marlon! The skeleton's ever so angry, and he's gone out of his castle, and he's got a shadowy thing with him, and they're going to find giants! Giants! Whatever shall we do?"

At the same moment, a loud clear voice boomed, "Marcus? Is that you? Goodness! Look, Hortense! There's Gracie Gillypot! And who's that lying on the ground? Has there been an accident?"

Chapter Twenty-three

Alf was right. Fiddleduster Squint was angry—angrier than he had ever been before. As the little bat flew in on his spying mission, he had found Fiddleduster storming around the confines of his castle, spitting and chewing at his own bony wrists.

"Pride! Such pride! The fall must be great . . . there must be fire and ruin, death and destruction of all that they hold dear. But how? But how?" He tore his claw-like fingernails down the mossy green wall, leaving deep gashes of white stone. "Even so, would I, Fiddleduster Squint, tear them limb from limb . . . but the border! I cannot cross the border!" He turned and slashed at the wall for a second time. "If their palaces could tumble and fall, crushing them beneath the heavy weight of iron and stone—"

Fiddleduster stopped. For a moment he was still. Gradually his face took on an expression of ferocious cunning, and he licked his bloodless lips. "The giants . . ." he murmured. "The giants! Walking mountains they may be . . . but their brains are small. They know nothing. They live and breathe and eat and drink, but think? No. They do not think, so hollow are their minds. But if something were to creep, to slide, to slither in their ear and whisper, 'Walk, dear Greatover! Walk, dear Meggymould! Walk, dear Trunkly . . . walk, walk, and do not stop. Walk, then run, then stamp . . . stamp and stamp and STAMP again . . .'" Fiddleduster Squint began to rock with mirthless laughter.

Up in a dark crevice, Alf had shivered as he listened.

"Yes! YES! The giants will shake the kingdom, set it shaking and quaking as never before, and every building will be dust, rubble, and ruin." Fiddleduster's eyes gleamed. "I will be avenged! If the prince of the kingdom cannot love my music, then he shall be squashed and crushed, even as a soft green grape is squashed and crushed by a hobnailed boot. Shadow! Come with me!"

And Fiddleduster loped away, his shadow at his heels.

Alf, gazing in horrified fascination, had suddenly remembered his instructions.

"Wowee!" he said to himself as he flew to report his findings. "Wowee!"

The giants, happily unaware of any oncoming danger, were wandering slowly in the direction of the Five Kingdoms, picking nuts and berries as they went. From time to time, Trunkly would ask hopefully, "IS WE NEAR EGGSIES HOUSES?" and Greatover would shake his enormous head.

"EGGSIES HOUSES IS FAR," he explained. "WILL FIND TOMORROW."

Trunkly rubbed her stomach. "TRUNKLY'S TUMBLY IS RUMBLY FOR EGGSIES. TRUNKLY RUN!" She did her best, but after only ten or eleven paces, she was puffed out and red in the face. "OOF! RUNNING IS TOO HARD FOR TRUNKLY."

"NO RUN." Greatover was firm. "TOO HARD FOR GIANTS. GO SLOW. SLOW AND STEADY. SLEEP SOON, THEN EGGSIES TOMORROW."

Such was the length of their stride, even a slow and steady pace took the three giants a long, long way before the sun began to sink over the distant mountains. The hills surrounding the Five Kingdoms were clearly visible when Greatover announced it was time to rest, and Trunkly smiled as she looked at them.

"TRUNKLY HAPPY!" she said, and she did a little jig to prove it. Birds, rudely awoken and shaken off their nighttime perches, scattered across the evening sky, and every door and window in the House of the Ancient Crones rattled.

The china, now tidily stowed in a locked cupboard, was safe enough, but Edna's evening cup of hot chocolate rocked wildly on its saucer. "Hmm," she said as she steadied it. "Let's hope they settle down again soon. Val's nerves are in pieces, and Elsie's not her usual self. Still, no point in worrying." She yawned. "Shall I have another look at the web before I go to bed? No. I'm too tired, and who knows what'll happen tomorrow. Elsie'll call me if anything changes." And the Ancient One was just in time to catch the sugar bowl as another enormous tremor sent it sliding across the table.

Fiddleduster Squint knelt down and felt the vibrations under his hand. "South-southwest," he muttered. "Oh, my sweet music. How I will be avenged."

Chapter Twenty-four

Hortense was shocked to find her cousin lying on the ground and fussed over him with what even Albion felt to be a suitable level of alarm. He immediately treated her and Queen Bluebell to a high-pitched account of all the terrible things that had happened to him that day, leaving them with a confused impression of ghostly shapes, candles in the dark, and howling banshees that had tipped him out of the wheelbarrow after bopping him on the head.

Gracie did her best to make things clearer, but she was distracted by having half heard Alf's news and knowing that it was urgent.

Marcus was rubbing his arms and feeling horribly mistreated; Marlon, seeing that both the queen and the duchess were distracted by Albion's tales of woe, flew silently onto his shoulder. "Kid," he whispered, "we've got trouble! There's a mighty angry zombie out there, and he's after revenge!"

Marcus, using the excuse of moving the wheelbarrow out of the way to inspect the damage, took several steps along the path. "What? What's happened?"

Alf came fluttering down to land on Marcus's other shoulder. "He's gone to find some giants!" he squeaked. "He wants to squish and squash the kingdoms like a plum! Or was it a grape? Or a—"

"GIANTS?" Marcus all but fell over his own feet in shock. "Did you say GIANTS?"

"Unc told me to watch and listen," Alf said, not without pride. "So I did. And the skeleton thing was ever so, ever so angry, and he's going to get giants to jump and thump and squish and squash—"

"Hold it right there, kid." Marlon sounded grim. "We get the picture—"

"What picture?" Gracie had slipped away, leaving Albion demonstrating his many bumps and bruises to his cousin and the queen.

Marcus was still absorbing the information. "Alf's trying to tell me there's a skeleton out there who's trying to get a herd of giants to come and flatten the Five Kingdoms."

"He's no skeleton," Marlon told him. "He's a zombie.

Or half-zombie. One of the bad 'uns, too, by the looks of him. And your Prince Albion trod on his toes—"

"I know what happened! I heard it! I heard it all!" Alf was twittering so fast that Marcus and Gracie could hardly understand what he was saying. "He's called Fiddleduster Squint, and he wants to get revenge by squishing—"

"SHUT IT, kid!" Marlon snapped, and Alf was finally silent.

Marcus leaned on the wheelbarrow, his mind whirling. "Let me get this right. There's a zombie out there, and he's after Albion? Just because Albion didn't like his music?"

"It wasn't like ordinary music," Gracie told him with a shiver. "It . . . it kind of twisted your brain and made everything inside you hurt."

"But . . ." Marcus shook his head in disbelief. "But why is it so dangerous? Zombies can't get across the border, can they? And Albion certainly isn't going to go wandering outside the kingdoms. He practically has a heart attack if anyone even mentions the wilderness!"

Marlon sighed. "You're right, kiddo. The zombie can't get across—not unless someone gives him an invite, and nobody in their right mind'll do that. But giants are something else."

"Giants can cross the border?" Marcus asked incredulously. "Surely not?"

"They don't need to. If Alf's right——"

"I am!" The squeak was indignant.

Marlon ignored the interruption. "If Alf's right, no giant would need to get across. They get within miles, and there's an earthquake. Buildings crashing, walls collapsing into rubble . . ."

"I see." Marcus scrubbed at his hair. "So they need to be stopped before they get too close."

Gracie leaned forward. "Now I know who the shadow belongs to," she said. "I knew it was evil. You should have seen Marley's face. He was absolutely green with fear, and he did exactly what the shadow told him. If Fiddleduster Squint's shadow is that scary, what must Fiddleduster himself be like?"

"He's a skeleton." Alf was not going to be left out. "He's a skeleton, and he plays the fiddle, which is what the prince didn't like and what——"

"OK, Alf." Marcus had heard enough. "We have to stop him."

"You're right." Gracie glanced over her shoulder. The duchess was still bent over Albion, but Queen Bluebell was straightening her shawl and looking around. "We ought to go at once . . . but what about

Albion and the queen and the duchess? We can't just leave them." She pointed at the wheelbarrow. "And that's useless now. You'll have to ride for help, Marcus. I don't see how we can do it any other way."

"I know!" Alf flew an overexcited figure eight. "Mr. Prince who isn't Mr. Prince is coming! He told me he was coming! And he's got soldiers with him—"

Seeing Gracie's blank expression, Marlon translated for her. "The twin, kiddo. Alf says he's heading for the palace."

"Arry?" Marcus's eyes widened. "Are you sure? And you've been talking to him, Alf?"

"Sure as eggs is eggs, Mr. Prince."

Marcus seized Gracie's hand. "That's it! Alf can go and get Arry and the soldiers . . . What on EARTH is he up to?" He shook his head. "Doesn't matter. We'll tell Her Maj and the duchess we're going for help, but as soon as we're out of sight, we'll head for the border instead!" Seeing Gracie's doubtful expression, he added, "It'll be all right! Truly!"

"What's all right? The wheelbarrow? Doesn't look all right to me." As Bluebell strode toward them, Marlon and Alf fluttered into the undergrowth. "I don't see much hope of getting young Albion home in that!"

Marcus stepped forward to make his speech about

riding for help but found he was quite unable to begin. There was something about Queen Bluebell's straightforward approach to life that made it difficult to lie. Even a mere twisting of the truth felt wrong. *And I bet I'm suffering from Gracie's Trueheart effect as well,* he thought. *Oh, bother!*

Bluebell stood watching as Marcus visibly struggled to find an explanation. "Anything you want to tell me?" she asked, and then, in what she fondly considered to be a whisper, "I can keep a secret, you know. Couldn't help noticing you and Gracie were having a bit of a chat. What's up?"

Arioso's words suddenly floated back into Marcus's mind. *Bluebell likes you . . .*

He took a deep breath. "Can we tell you something, ma'am? You won't faint, or anything?"

Bluebell snorted. "Faint? My dear boy, what sort of woman do you take me for?"

"Well . . ." Marcus looked at Gracie, and she gave him a nod of encouragement. "Well . . . we've heard about a . . . a dangerous situation. A threat. It's outside the Five Kingdoms, and it can't come in, but it might . . . it might cause some damage. If Gracie and I go right now this minute, we may be able to stop it. But that would mean leaving—"

"Leaving Albion with no way of getting back home," Bluebell finished his sentence. "I see. That does indeed present a difficulty."

"My brother's on his way," Marcus said quickly, wondering if the queen was in a state of shock, although she showed no visible signs of being anything of the kind. "Honestly, he'll be at the palace any time now, and Alf's going to take him a message—"

"Alf?" The queen peered around. "Who's Alf?"

The irrepressible Alf burst out from the bushes. "ME! I'm a messenger bat, and the prince who isn't our Mr. Prince, the other one, he had a chat with me this morning, and—"

Bluebell neither screamed, fainted, nor went pale. Instead she pulled out her lorgnette and inspected the little bat with interest. "A messenger bat, eh? How very useful. And you know Prince Arioso? Well, I'd say that solves the problem nicely. You fetch him along here and tell him to bring a couple of healthy, strapping lads with him. Hortense and I will stay with Albion and try and keep him from having a temper tantrum until help comes."

Alf did his best to salute in midair. "Yes, MA'AM!"

As he disappeared, Bluebell sighed. "How lovely to

have friends like that. I fear I missed a great deal in my youth. Make the most of it, my dears. Now, before you go, tell me. Seriously, should I be worried?"

"We hope not," Gracie began, and then, as if to demonstrate what could be about to happen, there was a rumbling in the far distance. The rumbling was followed by a faint shaking of the earth beneath their feet. It only lasted a few seconds, but there was no mistaking the fact that something singular had happened. There was a piercing scream from behind them, but Queen Bluebell only clasped her bag more tightly.

"Oh, dear," Gracie said. "I really think we'd better get on our way."

The queen raised an eyebrow. "Am I to assume that disturbance might be to do with your quest?"

"Yes," Gracie said simply. She hesitated, then ran to the old lady and gave her a loving hug. "Thank you for being so understanding. We really must go . . . but I promise we'll tell you everything as soon as we get back."

"So I should hope." Bluebell pulled out a large red handkerchief and blew her nose loudly. "Excuse me. I'm a silly old woman. But I do love a bit of bravery!"

Marcus stood to attention. "On behalf of myself and Miss Gracie Gillypot," he said formally, "I thank you, ma'am. There is no doubt in my mind that you are . . . you are one of the absolute BEST!"

Bluebell received this formality in the spirit in which it was meant. She curtsied low before shaking Marcus's hand with much warmth. "Dear boy. Dear, dear boy. Look after that girl of yours. She's worth her weight in gold."

Marcus grinned. "I know," he said. "I absolutely do."

"Be off with you, then." Bluebell blew her nose for a second time. "And good luck!"

Marcus nodded, then put his fingers in his mouth and whistled. Hinny, who had been peacefully cropping grass, came trotting toward him. Marcus held a stirrup until Gracie had settled herself in the saddle, then swung himself up behind her. He raised one arm in salute, then sent the pony cantering down the track that led to the Howling Arms and the wilderness beyond.

"What?" There was an outraged shriek from Albion. "What's going on? Where are they going? They can't leave me! They CAN'T! Marcus! Come back right now, this minute —"

"Albion?" Bluebell's best boom echoed up and down the path. "Are you a prince or a pretzel? Be quiet. Hortense, my dear, I have something important to tell you!"

Chapter Twenty-five

Prince Arioso had not enjoyed the journey to Cockenzie Rood. Gubble was not a talkative companion, but he was a very wet one, and Arry was all too conscious of the fact that he was sitting in a puddle of mud. As they drew up outside the palace, Gubble grunted. "Where Marcus?"

"I've no idea," Arry said. "But I'm sure the duchess will have more information." He turned to the four soldiers accompanying him and waved them away. "You can wait in the guardhouse." The soldiers obeyed with alacrity, hoping for tea and cake, and Arry began to climb out of the carriage. He was surprised to find Gubble reluctant to follow him. "Aren't you coming?"

Gubble looked suspiciously at the guardhouse. "Soldiers," he said. "Soldiers here not like Gubble."

"You'll be perfectly safe with me," Arry assured him. Gubble still didn't move, his small piggy eyes swiveling anxiously from the guardhouse to the palace and back again. The prince, somewhat to his own astonishment, put a comforting hand on the troll's grubby green foot. "Honestly, Gubble. It'll be all right. I'll look after you until we find Marcus."

Reassured, Gubble half jumped, half tumbled onto the ground. "Ug."

Together they walked to the front door. It was wide open, but Arioso was far too polite to follow Bluebell's example and stride inside. He rang the bell, but it took several attempts before a maid appeared. The sight of Gubble made her blink nervously, but Arry's evident respectability made her drop a quick curtsy.

"I'm really sorry, sir," she apologized, "but the butler's been dismissed, and we're all at sixes and sevens because His Majesty's away and Her Grace went out this morning and she didn't leave no instructions. Would you like to come in and wait?"

"Is Prince Albion available?" Arry asked.

The maid shook her head. "Not sure as he's even up yet, sir. He hasn't eaten any breakfast."

"Oh." Doubtful as to what should be his next move, Arry rubbed his nose. "Erm . . . so he hasn't been kidnapped, then?"

"Kidnapped?" The maid stared at him. "Who would want to kidnap His Highness?"

Gubble, dimly beginning to understand that Arioso was a very different character from Marcus, decided it was time to help. "Look for prince. Look NOW!"

His intention had been to suggest it was time to go searching for Marcus, but both Arry and the maid looked at the troll as if he was a genius. "Of course!" Arry said. "That's it! Well done, Gubble!"

The maid dropped another curtsy and scurried away, leaving the prince and the troll on the doorstep. Moments later she was back, accompanied by a smart young manservant. "This here's the prince's valet," she explained. "He says the prince went out early, and he hasn't been seen since." She began to cry. "So he HAS been kidnapped, then!"

Arioso's heart sank. "Erm . . . well . . ."

"He might have gone for a walk, sir," the valet suggested, and then, more quietly, "Hush, Susan! Nobody'd ever kidnap His Highness. Not unless they was paid a million, that is."

"A walk! Of course!" Arry cheered up at once. "That's

what he'll be doing. Come along, Gubble. Let's go and see. Erm . . . where does the prince like to walk?"

"He was in the vegetable garden yesterday," the valet offered. "Had carrots thrown at him. So he said. All his imagination, if you ask me."

Arry frowned at this disloyalty and took Gubble's hand. "We'll go and see for ourselves. Thank you."

As he walked away, Arry heard the valet remark, "Odd doings round here, Susan. That there troll was here yesterday! And so was that young man, but he weren't nearly so hoity-toity and high-and-mighty then. Still got dirty pants, though . . ."

Arioso, heir to the kingdom of Gorebreath, held his head high as he and Gubble took themselves around the corner. Half of him was resolving never to keep company with a troll again, but the kinder half couldn't help but be touched by the confidence with which Gubble looked up at him. "Find Marcus soon? And Gracie?"

"I'm sure we will," Arry promised. "Erm . . . where would we find the vegetable garden, would you think?"

"Looking for a cabbage, Mr. Prince who isn't?"

The voice was cheery and familiar, and Arioso sighed. "Oh," he said. "It's you again."

"Bat!" Gubble, unlike his companion, was delighted to see Alf. "Where Gracie?"

Alf demonstrated a super-straight A-line dive. His intention was to land on Arry's shoulder, but the prince, unused to such familiarity, moved swiftly aside, and Alf was forced to do a backflip and land on Gubble's head. "Mr. Prince and Miss Gracie are off on a really big adventure to find a skeleton in the wilderness who's ever so, ever so angry," he reported. "And can you bring your soldiers and follow the wheel tracks and collect the other prince, the one in the wheelbarrow, 'cause he's hurt and he can't get—"

The end of Alf's sentence was cut off by the sudden removal of his perch. Gubble had heard enough. He dropped Arry's hand, squinted up at the sun, and set off muttering, "Gubble go wilderness," under his breath.

Alf found an alternative perch on a nearby statue and tried again. "Soldiers," he repeated. "Mr. Prince—" Alf shut his eyes and made a supreme effort. "Mr. MARCUS Prince needs you, and he said for me to tell you 'cause we've met and you talked to me." He opened his eyes and saw Arry was still looking confused. "PLEASE, Mr. P. who isn't Mr. P.," he begged. "Go and get your soldiers to carry the prince!" An inspired thought came to him. "If you do, you'll be a HERO!"

There could not have been a better way to appeal to Arioso. The idea of being a hero without having to

fight any battles or do anything else that might involve messiness or unpleasantness was most appealing. Nina-Rose had been much on his mind; the thought that he could present himself to her in such a role (a role he had always thought to be way beyond his abilities) was compelling. "Absolutely," he said. "Follow the wheel tracks, you say? Right." The image of himself triumphantly escorting Albion back to his palace floated tantalizingly before his eyes. "THAT'LL show that valet. Humph!" And he hurried away.

Alf hesitated. Should he wait and check to see that all was done according to instructions? With some regret, he decided he should. "Responsible, that's what you are, Alf Batster," he told himself. "Responsible. Miss Gracie'll be proud of you."

It was not until Arioso and all four soldiers were well on their way that the little bat felt he could leave them to their own devices. Sailing up into the evening sky, he flew a wide circle, glancing down from time to time to see what was going on. Albion was still recumbent, but the duchess was sitting on a fallen tree and chatting amiably to Queen Bluebell. As Alf flittered past, he heard the duchess say, "Don't worry, Bluebell. There'll be NO surprises on your birthday. No surprises at all. I've had the most excellent idea.

You must celebrate—" The rest of her sentence was lost as Alf circumnavigated a flock of starlings flying home to roost. The little bat grinned to himself as he glanced back; Albion was wildly waving his arms, but it was too far away to tell if he was happy or angry.

"Better move on," Alf told himself. "Better find Miss Gracie and Mr. Prince." He took a more direct line; immediately below him Gubble's progress could be tracked by flattened bushes and trees bent at odd angles. Where other travelers were forced to circumvent walls or fences, Gubble went straight through. The Howling Arms had evidently had the misfortune to lie in his way; a large figure that Albion would have recognized as Gruntle Marrowgrease was standing outside and staring at a gaping hole, his whole stance registering stunned disbelief. Of Gubble himself there was no visible sign. Alf flew on and was pleased to find that Marcus and Gracie had already crossed the border. They were now on foot, picking their way up a steep and stony slope; Hinny was following them, stepping in and out of a tumbling creek. As he fluttered toward them, Alf could hear Marlon squeaking encouragement.

"Not far now," he was calling. "Up to the top and you'll see for miles!"

Alf twittered a greeting and swooped to join him.

Chapter Twenty-six

The messenger pigeon so unexpectedly released by Gubble was a bird with a very small brain. Arioso had chosen it for its attractive plumage, ignoring the pigeon master's gloomy prognostications of error and fatal mistakes. It had celebrated its freedom by heading straight for a field of peas, but after an hour or so of pleasurable eating had begun to wonder whether it was, perhaps, time to fly home. It took another while to make a decision. *Yes,* it thought, as it wandered round the pea field. *Yes. It's definitely time to go home.* And then, *But which home?*

The pigeon had been trained to fly between Gorebreath and Dreghorn, so was now in a state of severe confusion. It moved on to a field of barley while it considered the problem. Finally the call of a home roost became pressing and, with some difficulty, the bird took off and began flapping lazily toward Dreghorn. It arrived just as King Frank and Queen Mildred were taking their leave, having had a peaceful day with no mention of abductions or kidnappings. The queen had whispered to Princess Nina-Rose that Arry had very much wanted to come but had been sent on a special mission by his father. The princess inquired, with some interest, if it was very dangerous. When Queen Mildred said that she sincerely hoped not, Nina-Rose seemed disappointed rather than relieved but asked that Arry be given her love.

"So we're agreed?" Queen Kesta said as she kissed Mildred good-bye. "We'll hold the surprise party at Wadingburn, and darling Hortense will be there already, so all we have to do now is round up Horace and Tertius and dear little Fedora, although I don't think we'll ask Dowby because he won't come even if he's asked. And it's Cockenzie Rood Day, which is so annoying because dear sweet Albion will be busy all day, and I had hoped that he might like to sit next to sweet little Marigold because they'd make an absolutely lovely match, even though I hear she rather fancies Bluebell's funny little Vincent. And we'll bring the cake. Eighty-one candles! It'll be quite a sight!"

King Frank was yawning. He had dined well and

was conscious of the first stirrings of indigestion. "Come along, Mildred old girl. Time to get home."

The pigeon, also suffering pangs of indigestion, decided to take a quick rest before heading for the pigeon loft and landed on top of the royal carriage. Queen Kesta was the first to notice it. "Oh! A darling pigeon. Someone must have sent us a message."

The coachman reached out a hand and caught the bird. "Gorebreath bird, by the look of it, Your Majesty." He inspected the container on the bird's leg and tossed the pigeon back into the air. "No message, though. Nothing at all."

Queen Mildred watched it flutter away with gradually increasing agitation. Was it really a Gorebreath bird? Could it have been a message from Arioso — a message that had gotten lost? Or could her darling boy have been in such difficulties that he had actually been prevented from writing and had sent the bird as an SOS? She hurried the king into the coach, and as soon as they were inside, she leaned forward. "Frank, dear, did you SEE that pigeon? I'm sure it was one of ours! Oh, what do you think it means?"

King Frank frowned. "Did wonder about it myself. But there was no message. Why would Arry send a bird with no message?"

His wife clasped her hands together. "I'm sure he wouldn't have sent it if everything was all right. I'm worried, Frank! What should we do?"

"There's only one answer to that," the king said firmly. "We must go to Cockenzie Rood and see for ourselves!"

The queen heaved a huge sigh of relief. "You're so right. It's been at the back of my mind all day, and when that pigeon arrived, I all but fainted on the spot. Oh, dear! You don't think it's a little late for a visit, do you? If nothing's wrong, Hortense will think it very strange . . . but I do so want to know if darling Arry is in any danger!"

"Not at all," King Frank declared. "Hortense won't mind an iota. And it'll put your mind at rest, my sweet. Can't have my little woman worrying all night."

Mildred gave him a fond look. "We can tell Hortense about the plans for Bluebell's party while we're there," she pointed out.

The king nodded. "Good plan all around." He gave the coachman his instructions, and as the coach began to roll away, the two of them settled back in the carriage to have a comfortable doze.

Seconds later they were shaken awake by the coach coming to a sudden and abrupt halt. The carriage door was flung open, and Princess Nina-Rose climbed in and flumped herself down beside an astonished King Frank.

"I couldn't help hearing what you said," she announced. "You do have terribly loud voices, you know, so it wasn't exactly eavesdropping. Mother didn't hear—she's ever so deaf—so she won't be in a panic. I told her you'd invited me to stay, but actually I'm coming with you to Cockenzie Rood. If anything's happened to my dearest darling Arry, I ought to be the first to know." She pulled an exceptionally small, lacy hankie out of her pocket and dabbed at her eyes. "We ARE practically engaged, after all. You don't mind, do you?"

There was no opportunity for the king or the queen to reply. Nina-Rose tapped on the roof of the carriage with her parasol to set it in motion once more, then fell back on the velvet cushions. "Tell me when we get there," she instructed, and a moment later had every appearance of being fast asleep.

Chapter Twenty-seven

Fiddleduster Squint had reached the foothills some
time before. He, too, had had to scramble up the shaley
slope, slipping and falling, then scrabbling his way up
once again, and by the time he reached the top, his
anger was fueled to the boiling point. He looked back
to where the turrets of the Royal Palace of Cockenzie
Rood caught the last light of the setting sun and shook
his fist. "This time tomorrow," he threatened, "that
will be rubble. Rubble and the shrieking ghosts of
those who are crushed beneath the ruins."

"Rubble and ruins, Master," the shadow echoed.

Fiddleduster swung around to stare ahead. Night
mists were creeping over the wilderness, and it was
difficult even for someone habitually used to darkness
to see clearly what lay below and beyond the hills that
edged the Five Kingdoms. The shadow stayed close

to his master, saying nothing. At last the zombie gave a long, low whistle. "Over there, Shadow," he said, pointing with a long bony finger. "Do you see? They are farther than one could wish, but we should be there by dawn."

The shadow was uncertain if he was studying the bodies of reclining giants or the gentle swell of a cluster of hills, but as he stared, he realized he could make out the faintest rise and fall, as of breathing. "I see them, Master."

"Then, let us move on. We must be there before they wake, or our chance will be lost for another day. If we are fortunate, they will sleep beyond first light . . ."

As Fiddleduster strode on, the shadow hesitated. Had he heard a distant clatter of falling stones? Should he tell his master there was a possibility they were being followed? He listened again but could hear nothing. Resolving to be more vigilant in the future, he hurried to take his place beside his master.

The shadow had been right. Marcus had made an attempt to ride Hinny up the slope, but the pony had been unable to get any kind of foothold on the loose sliding stones, and the result had been a small landslide.

"We'll have to go on foot," Gracie whispered.

"OK," Marcus agreed, and then, "Why are you whispering?"

Gracie put her finger on her lips. "Look at Marlon."

Marcus looked up and saw Marlon hovering high above them, a minute black speck in the twilight. "What's he doing?"

"He's seen something odd," Gracie told him. "Shh! He'll be down to tell us if he thinks it's dangerous."

Sure enough, Marlon came dropping like a stone only moments later. "Want the bad news or the bad news?"

"Is it very bad?" Gracie asked.

Marlon considered. "Could be worse. Could be plagues of rats. Or snakes. Nah . . . the zombie's already at the top of the hill, and he's spotted the giants. They're asleep. Reckon he's aiming to reach them before sunup, so you'll have to travel all night if you're gonna have any chance of catching him."

"Is there any way of getting Hinny up the hill?" Marcus asked. "If we took turns riding, we'd travel faster."

The bat flew a wide circle. "Maybe," he reported on his return. "There's a stream on your left. Worth a try."

Gracie was twisting the end of her braid while she

tried to think of an alternative plan. "If only we could slow him down . . . but I can't think how. Or we could warn the giants . . . Would they listen to you, Marlon?"

"Nah. They don't hear bats. Fact."

"There's nothing else we can do." Marcus stood up. "Let's find this stream and do the best we can. It'll be dark soon. Marlon, can you show us the way?"

"Sure thing, kiddo. Follow me."

As Marlon flitted in front, Gracie and Marcus followed him, Marcus leading Hinny. The stream was some five hundred yards away; it meandered down the hill, cutting a twisted course through the slither of the shale. The prince and the pony splashed into the shallow water, and Marcus announced that it was much easier walking. "It's mostly sand and larger stones," he said. "The water's freezing, though."

Gracie, grateful for her oversize rubber boots, stepped into the stream after him. Steadily they climbed the hill; from time to time, they tried to walk along the bank but were driven back into the stream by the shifting stones and the unreliability of the footholds.

By the time Alf swooped down to join them, they had arrived at the top, where scrubland and stunted

gorse were interspersed with clumps of windswept trees. The sun had set, and there was only the faintest glimmer of light in the western sky.

As Gracie looked up, a star twinkled back at her, but even as she watched, it was extinguished by a bank of heavy clouds. She shivered. "It's very misty," she said. "I can't see anything. It's a good thing we've got you and Alf, Marlon." She smiled at the bats and then went on, "I was wondering . . . I don't know if it's possible to do it in time, but I just thought I'd ask . . . how long would it take to fly to the House of the Ancient Crones, do you think?"

"Never get there and back by morning, kid," Marlon said. "Don't think I haven't checked it out, neither. Why d'you ask?"

"I keep getting a weird feeling about what we're doing," Gracie told him. "I suppose I just wanted to know if Auntie Edna had any good ideas. I mean, how do you stop a giant?"

Marcus snorted. "Trip it up?"

Alf tittered, but Gracie went on with her line of thought. "Why should they listen to us, anyway? I don't know anything about them . . . only that Auntie Edna once had a friend who was a giant. She gets sad when she talks about him."

"There's your answer, kiddo." Marlon landed on her shoulder. "If the Ancient had a giant as a pal, they have to be OK."

"So why will they listen to Fiddleduster Squint?" Gracie shivered again. "Yeuch. Even thinking about him makes me feel cold. And a bit sick."

Marcus put a comforting arm around her shoulders. "Maybe they won't take any notice of him."

"Maybe. But I'm sure he's got some kind of hideous plan." Gracie took a deep breath. "So we'd better go and find out what it is."

There was a sudden small squeak from close beside her. "I'll go, Miss Gracie. To the Ancient Crones. I'm ever so fast, you know! Even Unc says I am! Don't you, Uncle Marlon? Just watch me, watch me fly! Wheeeeeeeeee!"

"Alf! NO!" Gracie called in alarm. "Alf? Alf, come back! It's too far."

There was no answer.

Marlon sighed. "No telling 'im," he said, but Gracie could hear pride in his voice. "Flip, flap, fly, and off they rush. That's young 'uns for you. We'd better be off as well. This way, kiddos!"

Chapter Twenty-eight

Prince Arioso was feeling remarkably pleased with himself. He had effected the rescue of a fellow prince and was now being feted and applauded in the Royal Palace of Cockenzie Rood. It was true that the rescue had not been especially dramatic, and Arry would be the first to admit that he himself had not made any attempt to carry the moaning Albion, but who had provided the soldiers who had had that privilege? He had. And who was it who had stepped out from the trees and declared, "Fear not, Prince Albion. Help is at hand!"? It was true that Albion had not uttered a single word of thanks and had sulked all the way back to the palace, but the duchess and Queen Bluebell had more than made up for his rudeness.

And then . . . then had come the ultimate accolade. As they were finishing a celebratory dinner, there had been the rumble of wheels outside. A servant had been dispatched to see who could possibly be calling so late in the evening and had returned to announce not only his father and mother, but his beloved Princess Nina-Rose.

The duchess was seldom at a loss in a social situation. "What a very unexpected delight!" she said. "Do ask them to come and join us!"

Nina-Rose, pausing only to check her appearance in the hall mirror, was first through the door. She rushed to Arioso and flung her arms around him. "Darling Arry!" she cooed. "Are you wounded?"

"Of course he isn't." Albion, slumped in a chair at the head of the table, spoke for the first time. "It's me who's wounded. Bopped, battered, bruised, and then deserted." He glared at Queen Mildred. "If it wasn't for Arry, I'd still be lying out there in the cold, wet grass." He gave a self-pitying sigh. "In fact, I'd probably be dead by now for all that some people cared."

"Oh, Arry!" Nina-Rose kissed him fondly. "What a hero you are!"

Queen Bluebell peered at Albion over her lorgnette. "Excuse me, young man," she said. "As far as I'm aware, your cousin and I never left your side."

"Yes, you did." Albion stuck out his lower lip. "You

went to talk to Marcus and that girl, Gracie Frillypot or whatever her name is."

This was more than Bluebell could bear, and she stood up to protest. At the same moment, King Frank came puffing into the room, and good manners required that she restrain herself. With an effort, she sat down again.

"Evening, Hortense," the king said as he sank into a chair. "Sorry to barge in on you like this. Mildred and I got in a bit of a flap, doncha know. Looks like it's all OK, though. See young Albion's safe and sound, after all!"

"No, I'm not." Albion frowned. "I'm hurting all over. I was bopped on the head and then kidnapped and wheeled away in a barrow to be tortured by horrible noises."

King Frank and Queen Mildred stared at him, openmouthed.

Nina-Rose gave a little cry of horror. "Poor, poor little Albie! But darling Arry found you and rescued you, didn't he?"

"I escaped first." Albion nodded hard. "Yes. I escaped, and I ran very very fast until my legs wore out. And then I met Gracie Frillypot and Marcus, and Marcus wheeled me back in the barrow—"

"MARCUS?" The king and the queen spoke together.

"Yes. Marcus wheeled me, but he bumped me on all the stones before he tipped me out and the wheelbarrow broke, and then he and Gracie rode away and left me. Abandoned me! Didn't even say good-bye!"

There was a horrified silence, finally broken by Nina-Rose. "And THEN darling Arry found you and rescued you?"

Albion gave a grunt of agreement. "Yes."

Bluebell took a deep breath. "I would like to say that dear Hortense and I met Albion, Marcus, and Gracie quite by chance just after the unfortunate accident with the wheelbarrow occurred. At no point was Albion left on his own and, far from abandoning him, Marcus took every care to make sure he was rescued. A messenger was sent to Prince Arioso. Isn't that the case, Arry?"

"Erm . . . yes. Yes, I did get a message." Arry nodded.

"And THAT'S when you rushed to Albie's side." Nina-Rose gazed at her prince with adoring eyes.

"It's all quite true," the duchess said, aware that the king was frowning heavily. "You mustn't blame Marcus."

"I do," Albion said promptly. "He went off, even

though I begged and begged and BEGGED him not to!"

Queen Mildred looked anxiously at her husband, who was beginning to mutter to himself. "Dearest," she said, "isn't it wonderful that darling Arioso has been so brave? And we don't know what Marcus was thinking. I'm sure he would never have ridden away unless he had a very good reason."

"If you ask me," the king said, and it was obvious that he was keeping his temper with great difficulty, "that boy NEVER thinks! Does exactly what he likes, when he likes. Takes no notice of me or anybody else. He's a disgrace. A total disgrace! Oh, I know he's had the odd lucky moment in the past and sorted out a few things here and there, but his behavior is intolerable. INTOLERABLE! Look at him yesterday. Asleep! Asleep, while his brother was making a speech! And then what does he do? He runs away. And today? He disobeys all my orders and runs off yet again! He's gone too far this time, by thunder, he has! MUCH too far!" He banged the table with his fist, making the plates and glasses jump. "I've a very good mind to disown him. No, Mildred! Don't say a word! I mean it. From this moment on, Marcus is no longer a prince of Gorebreath!"

Even Albion was shocked by this outburst. Nina-Rose

clutched Arry's hand, and the duchess and Queen Mildred looked at each other in silent concern. Queen Bluebell put down her lorgnette and rose to her feet.

"Frank," she said, "you're a fool. That boy Marcus is worth all the rest of us put together. He has more courage in his little finger than you have in your whole body, and if he was my son, I'd be singing his praises to the rooftops. Now I know you're angry, and when you calm down, you'll most likely regret what you've just said and change your mind, but remember this—if ever you disown young Marcus, I shall claim him as my own. Vincent's my heir, but he's a ninny, and his sister can't bear the idea of being queen. Let me tell you something, Frank. If I thought Marcus would agree to be king of Wadingburn, I'd die happy. So there. Put that in your pipe and smoke it!" And the queen stalked out of the dining room, her very backbone rigid with disapproval.

This time the silence was so long that two of the maids thought the room was empty and whisked in to clear the dishes. Seeing the entire royal party sitting frozen to their seats, they hurriedly withdrew. The interruption served to break the tension, however, and the duchess did her best to save the evening. "I'm so sorry," she said. "I never thought to ask if you would care for something to eat. Would you like a little lemon mousse, perhaps? Or a cup of tea?"

"I rather think we ought to go, Hortense dear," Queen Mildred said, and she began to fuss with her bag.

"But we CAN'T!" Nina-Rose turned to her. "You wouldn't drag darling Arry away, would you? He's a hero! We should drink to his health!"

Albion coughed meaningfully.

"Oh, yes." Nina-Rose waved a hand. "And I suppose it wouldn't hurt to drink to poor little Albie's health as well. Here's to them both!"

King Frank dithered. Should he go, or should he stay? He had been deeply offended by Bluebell's speech, but on the other hand she had had the sensitivity to leave the room. No doubt she was even now repenting her tirade. He himself was aware that he might, just might, have gotten a little carried away in the heat of the moment. And the Royal Palace of Cockenzie Rood was very comfortable, and it was a long, long drive home.

He made up his mind. "Well said, Nina-Rose. Here's to Prince Albion and Prince Arioso! And well done, Arry. I'm proud of you. Very proud, indeed."

The royal party relaxed, although Albion continued to cast dark and meaningful looks at the duchess.

Queen Mildred heaved a sigh of relief. "Oh!

Hortense!" she said. "I'd almost forgotten! We were at Dreghorn today, and Kesta has SUCH a lovely plan for Bluebell's birthday!"

The duchess paused over the teapot. "Might that be a surprise party?"

"You knew!" Mildred beamed. "Isn't it fun? We're all going to come to Wadingburn, with a huge cake with eighty-one candles on it!"

"But, Mildred . . . Bluebell won't be there." Hortense poured out the tea and handed the cups around. Albion, looking thunderous, pushed his cup away and scowled even more fiercely at his cousin, who went suavely on, "Didn't you know? She's coming here for her birthday."

The queen looked crushed. "Oh, no! But it's Cockenzie Rood Day! She won't be able to have her party!"

"I say, cuz," Albion said, a sudden ray of hope illuminating his extreme gloom. "I think that's a terrible shame! Why don't you go to Wadingburn, after all? You said you were going to, right up until today!"

"I'm sorry, Albion. It's all arranged." When the duchess spoke in that particular tone of voice, Albion knew better than to argue. With a shrug, he relapsed back into sulky silence.

Nina-Rose looked at the duchess in wide-eyed

astonishment. "But why can't Queen Bluebell have her party here at Cockenzie Rood instead?" she asked. "Albie sweetie, you wouldn't mind, would you? Don't you have a band or something like that? They could march up and down playing 'Happy Birthday to You.'"

"Lovely!" Queen Mildred clapped her hands. "And we can bring the cake here instead! How clever you are, Nina-Rose."

"Isn't she?" Arioso gazed rapturously at his beloved.

"Splendid plan." King Frank nodded. "So that's all sorted out. No need for you to worry anymore, Hortense."

Hortense was in a quandary. Bluebell had not wanted any fuss; was this worse or better than the dreaded surprise party?

"It does sound like an excellent idea," she said slowly, as she tried to think of a way to escape. "What do you think, Albion?"

Albion was pale, sweaty, and speechless. His dreams of a royal parade had been shattered by his cousin's announcement that Bluebell was to spend her birthday at Cockenzie Rood; now it seemed that hideous insult was going to be added to appalling injury. A marching band but not for him? A marching band, playing 'Happy Birthday' to Bluebell? What about his glorious uniform? His twenty wonderful scarlet cloaks? He staggered to his feet, holding his head. "I don't know why you even bother to ask me things like that," he said shrilly. "Nobody EVER listens to me or to what I want! It's not fair! I'm going to bed!" And he left as fast as his still-uncertain legs could carry him.

"Oh, dear," Hortense said. "I'd better go and see if he's all right. Please excuse me for a moment. He's had a horrid day, poor boy."

"No thanks to a certain young person of our acquaintance." King Frank gave his wife a meaningful nod. "Naming no names, of course."

The duchess gave him a quick glance but decided there was nothing more to be said for the moment. Hopefully a good night's sleep would see a change of heart. With a sigh, she rang a bell to order bedrooms to be prepared for her unexpected guests. Then, as the king and queen began to discuss birthday plans with Nina-Rose and Arioso, she slipped away to see to Albion. After that, she promised herself, she would take her very good friend Bluebell a cup of tea and have a sensible conversation.

The hours of the night ticked by. Trunkly was dreaming of her eggsies; from time to time, she stirred and smiled in her sleep. Meggymould and Greatover slept without moving, the enormous mounds of their bodies already suggesting the mountains they would eventually become. Fiddleduster Squint was moving steadily toward them, the cold light of revenge gleaming in his sunken eyes. From time to time, Marlon fluttered over his head, unseen in the misty darkness, before returning to where Gracie and Marcus were plodding wearily onward. Marcus had tried to persuade Gracie to ride Hinny, but she had insisted that they take turns; now, in an attempt to give the pony something approaching a rest, they were half running, half walking on either side of her, each holding a stirrup to prevent them from stumbling into sleep.

"What time do you think it is?" Gracie whispered.

Marcus stifled a yawn. "I'm not sure. Quite a long time after midnight, I'd say. Maybe three or four in the morning?"

"It feels as if we've been walking forever," Gracie said. "It can't be too long before the sun comes up." She squinted into the distance. Was it her imagination, or was the sky already a little lighter than it had been?

There was the faint whir of wings, and Marlon appeared. "Keep going, kiddos. Believe it or not, you're catching up. You're doing good."

"How much farther is it?" Marcus wanted to know.

"Maybe a coupla hours." Marlon thought it unnecessary to add that this was an optimistic guess. He, too, was tired, and he was unwilling to waste his strength flying far ahead to check on the exact location of the giants. It would be very obvious where they were as soon as it was light, and all Marlon's instincts were telling him that dawn was not far away. "Keep going. Like I say, you're doing good. Your uncle Marlon's proud of you!"

Had Marlon been able to see his nephew, he would have been proud of him too. The little bat was flying on the longest journey he had ever made, and his wings were aching. "Mustn't stop," he told himself. "Mustn't stop!" As the hours passed, he grew wearier and wearier, but apart from the briefest of rests after crossing the river Gore, he did not stop. At last, just as the sky was beginning to pale in the east, he flew over the trees of the Less Enchanted Forest. "Nearly there," he gasped, "nearly there!" And with one last heroic effort, he turned a victory roll before diving down the tallest chimney of the House of the Ancient Crones. With a whoop of self-congratulation, he zoomed out of the fireplace, startling Edna so much she dropped the shuttle of filigree silver

thread. With a cry of "Emergency! Emergency!" Alf collapsed in a tiny crumpled heap on the floor.

"Goodness me!" The Ancient One hastily picked up her shuttle, then bent to attend to the limp form of Alf. For once she was alone in room seventeen, and it was dangerous to leave the web of power for longer than a few minutes. Holding Alf tenderly, she hurried to the door. "Elsie!" she called. "Elsie! Could you come here?"

Elsie, wrapped in her bathrobe and looking cross and crumpled, appeared in a matter of seconds. "What is it?" she asked.

"It's Alf." The Ancient One stroked the bat's small furry back. "He's exhausted. He said there was an emergency and then fainted . . . could you take over the loom while I find some Restoration Liquor?"

Elsie looked doubtful. "Are you sure? Isn't it rather strong for such a very little one?" But she stepped over to the loom. Edna thanked her with a nod and made her way to a cupboard in the corner. Opening the door, she took out a small silvery bottle and shook a couple of drops into Alf's mouth.

For a moment there was no response, but then he sneezed, sat up, and looked around, his eyes shining brightly. "Oh! Hello, Mrs. Edna! Did you see me come down the chimney? I've been flying for miles 'n' miles 'n' miles 'n' MILES, and I did it! I came all the way from the hills and I got here— OH!" A distracted expression twisted his small face into a look of intense worry. "Am I too late? Have I been asleep? I shouldn't have been asleep—it's an emergency! Miss Gracie and Mr. Prince—they're rushing to catch a skeleton who wants to squash the kingdoms like a GRAPE!"

"Edna!" Elsie's tone was urgent. "Look at this . . . there are black spots all over the web."

The Ancient One went to see. "That'll be evil threatening the kingdoms but from the outside. Hmm. It's very close to the giants."

"That's the skeleton!" Alf was now fully recovered. With a flip of his wings, he was up on the top of the loom. "He's going to squish—"

"Alf!" Edna gave him an exasperated smile. "Could you explain just a little more? WHAT is this skeleton planning?"

Alf tucked his wings around him and began to tell his story. As he went on, the Ancient One looked more and more serious. "That's an awful lot for one Trueheart to deal with," she said. "I've heard of Fiddleduster Squint. He's evil. Deeply evil. And now Albion's upset him. Oh, dear."

Elsie nodded wisely. "The perils of rejecting an artist. Scorn them, and they release the inner tiger."

Edna ignored her. "We need to help . . . let me think."

Alf waved a wing. "I can fly back, Mrs. Edna! No problem!"

"I'm afraid it would take too long," the Ancient One said gently. "Even for such a speedy flyer as you. No—"

A tap on the window made all three of them look up in surprise. Edna held her candle higher, then chuckled. "Well, I never. That could be the answer—but is it reliable enough?"

"What? What are you talking about?" Elsie peered into the night. "I can't see anything!"

"It's the path," Edna told her. "It was knocking at the window."

Elsie gave a loud and disapproving sniff. "Huh! It was the path that caused this trouble in the first place! If it had taken Prince Marcus to Gorebreath, as it was told to, none of this would have happened."

"You can't blame the path for Fiddleduster Squint," the Ancient One pointed out. "And maybe it would like to make up for its mistakes . . . and it might be our only hope of getting help to Gracie in time."

"Help?" Alf squeaked. "Are you going to save her, Mrs. Edna?"

The Ancient One shook her head. "I can't, Alf. I can't leave the web of power. One day, hopefully, someone will come and take my place, but for now I have to watch, watch and weave." She bent down and with a sharp tug pulled a long gleaming thread from the spool of filigree. "But you can save her . . . you and Elsie."

"ME?" Elsie clutched at her chest. "But I haven't left the house for over seventy years!"

"I'll look after you, Mrs. Elsie," Alf reassured her. "And shall I look after the silvery string?"

Edna handed the thread to Elsie, who staggered, then recovered herself with an effort. "It's much too powerful for you, Alf, dear. Only a Trueheart, or"— she gave Elsie a quick nod—"someone whose heart is truly cleansed can carry its weight. Now, there's no more time for chitchat. Be off with you! And, Alf—you must tell the path where to go."

Elsie knotted her bathrobe belt more tightly, hung her wig on the end of the loom, and stood up straight. "I'm ready," she said.

Edna seated herself in front of the loom and picked up the silver shuttle. "Hurry back, dear."

"Of course," Elsie told her. "And I'll bring our girl with me. And her prince. After all, his pony's here waiting for him."

Alf had flittered to the door. "Come on, Mrs. Elsie!" he encouraged, and as Elsie stepped into the corridor, the floor tipped, sliding her down to the far end and the wide-open back door. As Elsie tumbled out into the cold night air, the house lurched, as if bidding her good-bye and good luck. With a squeal, she fell onto the waiting path, Alf close behind her.

"Here we go!" Alf squeaked. "Giddyup, Path! Alf and Mrs. Elsie to the rescue!"

Chapter Twenty-nine

The first rays of the sun were scratching at the sky as Fiddleduster Squint and his shadow reached the giants. All three were still sleeping; the ground trembled as Greatover snored, and the nearby birch trees swayed to and fro in the wind of Meggymould's breathing. Even Fiddleduster was taken aback by their size now that he was beside the giants, but his desire for revenge overcame any hesitation.

"Come," he whispered to his shadow. "Let us begin!"

"What shall I do, Master?" the shadow asked.

Fiddleduster cracked his knuckles as a ghoulish grin spread over his face. "You must creep into an ear, Shadow. And once there you must whisper, whisper of running. Running to the Five Kingdoms, running and running, and never thinking to stop—"

He paused as Trunkly stirred, rubbed her eyes, and turned over.

"EGGSIES," she murmured. "LUVVY EGG-SIES . . ." And then she was asleep again.

Fiddleduster's eyes lit up. "Eggs? She wants eggs? Go swiftly, Shadow. Whisper of eggs by the hundreds, by the thousands . . . eggs that must be seized without delay, or they will vanish! Vanish, leaving her hungry."

The shadow nodded and slithered its way up Trunkly's solid and dirt-encrusted neck. She grunted but did not wake. Sliding into the curve of her ear, Shadow began to whisper, and with a loud roar of "EGGSIES!" Trunkly rolled over and staggered to her feet. Lurching first one way and then the other, she stared wildly around, her eyes wide open but as yet unfocused. Meggymould and Greatover sat up and looked at her in surprise; Fiddleduster Squint slipped behind the birch trees. There he gathered his thoughts into one clear stream of instruction to his shadow. "Do not stop! Drive her into madness! Send her running . . . The others will follow!"

Marlon, flying into the early light, saw Trunkly's massive figure rise up against the paling clouds as if a mountain had burst out of the earth. He froze mid-wingbeat. "Holy moly!" he whispered, then zoomed down to where Marcus and Gracie were making as much speed as their exhaustion would allow. Even from their much lower perspective, Trunkly's head and shoulders towered over the horizon, and Marcus gasped.

Gracie put her hand over her mouth. "WOW!" she said. "WOW!"

"And that's only the little 'un," Marlon said grimly. "Come on, kiddos. Shake a leg."

Trunkly was now shambling in circles, clutching at her head. She could hear a buzzing in her ear, but the shadow's voice was too high-pitched for her to understand much of what he was saying. All she knew was that it was acutely uncomfortable and, in some way that she would never have been able to define, deeply evil.

"WHAT IS MATTER?" Meggymould asked anxiously. "WHAT TRUNKLY DOING?"

Fiddleduster was beginning to realize there was no point in subtlety. He shut his eyes and beamed the simplest of thoughts. "Louder! Tell her, RUN! NOW!"

The shadow did as he was told, and Trunkly screamed. Greatover and Meggymould caught at her hands and tried to soothe her, but she twisted away and began to run, shaking the ground at every step.

The ever-peaceful Hinny reared, trembling with fear, and Marcus and Gracie clutched at each other to stay upright.

Far, far away in the Royal Palace of Cockenzie Rood, every guest woke with a start as bedside teacups clattered in their saucers, pictures slid sideways, and windows rattled. Edna, in the House of the Ancient Crones, hung on to her loom as the floor pitched and swayed beneath her feet. Birds were shaken out of sleep, and animals ran distractedly that way and this, not knowing what to do.

Fiddleduster Squint was thrown back between the trees and lost any sense of connection with his shadow, but it made no difference. Trunkly had only one thought, and that was to get away from the horrible, evil thing hissing in her ear.

"She's running mad," Marlon reported as Gracie and Marcus recovered and began to hurry onward as best they could.

"Which way is she going?" Gracie panted.

"Every which way. Zigzagging— No! She's off!"

Marlon was right. Trunkly was now thundering in the direction of the Five Kingdoms. Worse still, Greatover and Meggymould had finally heaved themselves upright and were lumbering after her.

It was all but impossible for Marcus and Gracie to stay on their feet as the world rocked around them; Marcus was very pale, and Gracie's face was washed of all color. She could feel evil heavy in the air, but there was nothing she could do as the enormous figure of the giantess hurtled past.

A moment later the rising sun broke free of the early morning clouds. Sunlight beamed down, and a strange silver object moving among the thick scrub caught the first of the rays. The sharp reflected light dazzled Trunkly, temporarily blinding her. She shook her head, tripped, and fell headlong, sending shock waves for miles around. Marlon was tossed into a whirlwind and swept away, choking and fighting for breath. A swirling dust cloud engulfed Trunkly's fallen body and floated high in the air above her, blotting out the sunlight and turning the immediate world gray. Moments later Greatover and Meggymould blundered into view. Crouching down beside Trunkly's fallen mass, they began to murmur to her and stroke her hands and arms.

As soon as the ground had stopped shaking, Gracie and Marcus hurried forward. It was obvious that neither Meggymould nor Greatover had eyes for anything other than Trunkly, but Gracie was desperate to try and speak to them. Even though they were so very large, she felt no fear; there was a deep feeling of rightness about them and a simple but unshakable goodness. *They're just like huge old trees,* she thought.

As Gracie came closer, Meggymould reached over to brush the matted hair away from Trunkly's face, and the shadow shifted to crouch deeper. Gracie saw the movement and half saw, half felt the shadow's presence. It was whispering again, exhorting Trunkly to get back on her feet, cursing and swearing and hissing insults. Trunkly, her simple mind battered and bruised, was whimpering with pain and distress. Gracie clenched her fists and took a step nearer, and as she did so, she crossed the thought line between Fiddleduster and his shadow. At once the words buried themselves in Gracie's brain, and the shadow was left in silence. Trunkly stopped her whimpering and lay still.

"OUCH!" Gracie rubbed at her ears, then swung around—and found herself looking directly at Fiddleduster Squint as he stood framed between two birch trees. He was as shocked as she was, and for a long second they stared at each other, Gracie's head full of pain and swirling ugly words. With a sharp intake of breath, she put up all the resistance she was capable

of and saw from Fiddleduster's expression that he was the source of the evil, and that—for the moment—it had returned to him. His deep-set eyes were glittering, and he was staring at her with an unpleasant curl of his lip, revealing long, sharp teeth.

"What is it?" Marcus asked urgently. "What is it?" His gaze followed Gracie's, and he also saw Fiddleduster Squint. "Is he the one who's making the giant mad?"

Gracie nodded without speaking. She now knew that as long as she was between Fiddleduster and his shadow, there could be no communication, and Trunkly would be safe; Fiddleduster knew this, too, and was moving stealthily away from the trees. As he moved, so did Gracie, always keeping her eyes on him, and her body between him and Trunkly.

"So," Fiddleduster said softly, "one sees a Trueheart. Well, well, well. A Trueheart, outside the borders, and all alone."

"She's not alone! I'm here!" Marcus, thinking to protect Gracie, stepped in front of her. Immediately he was flung to his knees by the intensity of the stream of corruption and evil. "Attack her, and you'll have me to deal with!" He was still defiant.

Neither Fiddleduster nor Gracie dropped their stare.

The pain in Gracie's head was excruciating, but she kept her eyes fixed on the zombie.

"A mere boy?" Fiddleduster's withering contempt made Marcus flush. "What can you do? Watch me . . . watch me as I destroy the Trueheart. After that it will give me extreme pleasure to tear you limb from limb. And then the giants will be entirely in my power—"

"Ug," said a voice.

Gubble, a shining silver cup angled over one eye like a jaunty helmet, came stumping into view through the floating clouds of dust. Auntie Vera was fluttering beside him. Neither of them appeared to notice anything out of the usual. "Where Gracie?"

Fiddleduster Squint wavered . . . and turned to look.

Immediately Gracie seized her opportunity. She ran to Trunkly, and in front of the astonished Greatover and Meggymould hurled herself between the giantess's ear and the shadow. "There!" She pointed back at Fiddleduster Squint. "Don't let him near! He's poisoning Trunkly's mind! Help me—I can't stop him for much longer."

Greatover and Meggymould blinked. Something was wrong. Very wrong. There was a girl. A little person. That was certain. And this girl was helping their Trunkly. But how? As their ponderous minds began to slowly process the information, Marcus ran at Fiddleduster. "Come on! Stop him!"

At the same moment, the zombie darted toward Gracie. He and Marcus collided, and the zombie snarled and bit while Marcus shouted and punched and pummeled at the flailing arms and legs that seemed made of steel.

"UFF . . . ug!" Gubble had reached them. He wrapped his long green arms around Fiddleduster Squint and hauled him away from the prince, while Auntie Vera fluttered around his head. The strength of the zombie was extraordinary; even the troll was straining to hold him.

"Is badness!" Gubble muttered. "Bad badness!" His muscles were bulging as Fiddleduster writhed and squirmed, and sweat was trickling down his flat green face.

Gracie could feel the shadow moving behind her, and a memory of how it had attacked Albion made her wonder how long she could protect Trunkly. She shut her eyes and concentrated as hard as she could on the web of power, imagining its silver cloth wrapping her in its protective folds.

"Shadow!" Fiddleduster was screaming. "Shadow! Kill, Shadow, kill!"

Gracie felt a deathly coldness behind her, and Gubble began to pant. "Gubble . . . Gubble can't . . ."

"Hang on, Gubble! Hang on . . ." Gracie pleaded. "Oh, please! Please! Won't somebody help us?"

Greatover leaned forward, picked up a sharp-edged boulder, and plunged it into the earth. A deep crack split the ground, a fissure so deep it was impossible to see the bottom.

Gubble, gasping and purple with exertion, saw what had been done. With one last final effort, he lifted the zombie over his head and threw him into the gaping void. "Urf," he said, then fell flat on his back.

The shadow slithered out of Trunkly's ear, irresistibly drawn toward its master. As it slid past Gracie, it hissed, "We will return . . . We will return . . ." before slipping over the edge of the crevasse and vanishing into the darkness.

"Gone," Gubble said. "Badness all gone."

Gracie rubbed her face and looked up at Greatover. "Thank you," she shouted as loudly as she could. "Thank you so much! You saved us!"

"Thank you!" Marcus echoed. He was crouched near the birch trees that had sheltered Fiddleduster.

Greatover shook his heavy head. "YOU DID TRY TO SAVE OUR TRUNKLY." An enormous tear rolled down his cheek and plopped onto the ground beside Gracie. "POOR TRUNKLY."

Gracie turned to look. Trunkly was lying very still, but Gracie could see the long grass stirring by her mouth. "She's not dead," she said. "I think she's just exhausted. I can see her breathing."

Even as she spoke, Trunkly's eyes flickered and opened. "IS I DEAD?" Seeing Gracie, her eyes grew wider. "IS LITTLE PERSON!" A hopeful smile curved her lips. "LITTLE PERSON WITH EGGSIES?"

Gracie laughed in relief. "Eggs? Is that what you want? I'm sure we could find you some. Auntie Elsie's got far too many."

Meggymould also began to smile. "EGGSIES FOR TRUNKLY! WE IS HAPPY! TRUNKLY CAN DANCE—"

"NO!" Gracie's heart beat faster at the thought. "No—please don't dance! Well, not here. I'm so glad you're happy, but you do make the ground shake quite dreadfully. Perhaps you could sing, instead? What do you think, Marcus?"

There was no answer. Puzzled, Gracie looked

around. "MARCUS!" She jumped to her feet and ran to where the prince sat clutching his leg. "What is it? OH! You're hurt! You're bleeding—"

"That horrible thing bit me," Marcus said. "I feel a bit odd."

Gracie put her hand on his forehead and found it was burning. "You're boiling! I bet it's poisonous, a bite like that. We must get you help . . . Where's Marlon? Marlon!"

There was a faint squeak, and Marlon came fluttering down. He also looked very much the worse for wear, his usually spruce and shining fur dull and matted. "Got blown away," he explained. "Whirlwind. What's up, kiddo?"

"It's Marcus," Gracie said, doing her best not to let her voice shake. "We need to get him to the crones as soon as we can . . . It's urgent!"

"Urgent? What's urgent? Never fear, Alfie's here!" As Alf flew down, he was delighted to find so many eyes staring at him in astonishment. "Yeeha! And hello, all!" He flew a victory roll followed by a spiral and a double circle. "Oh! What's up with Mr. Prince?"

"Looks like a nasty case of zombie poisoning to me." As the path swooped and came to rest, Elsie stepped down as calmly as if she traveled in such a manner every day of her life. "Best get him home. Fast."

Gracie burst into tears. "I'm sorry," she sobbed as she fished in her pocket for a non-existent handkerchief. "Crying's such a useless thing to do — but I'm so pleased to see you, Auntie Elsie! I'm so worried about Marcus!"

Elsie smiled. "Hush, my love. Auntie Elsie's here now, so let's get busy. Gubble dear, you look dreadful! Do you feel you could lift young Marcus onto the path? Yes? That's good. And who have we here? Well, well, well. I'd say you must be Trunkly, Greatover, and Meggymould."

The three giants rumbled quietly. Things were happening far too fast for them to fully comprehend, but they accepted that they were surrounded by small people of good intent and were happy.

Gracie wiped her nose on her sleeve. "I said they could have some eggs, Auntie Elsie. Is that OK?"

"They can have the hens and henhouse too," Elsie said cheerfully. "I'm bored to death with the feeding and cleaning. We'll let the hens loose where the giants can find them easily. Somewhere well away from the Five Kingdoms." She paused to watch as Gubble lifted Marcus onto the path. "Well done,

Gubble. You'll be coming with us, of course. Now, what about that pony? Can't leave it on its own out here."

Auntie Vera fluttered forward. "I can guide her back," she offered. "As far as Cockenzie Rood Palace, anyway. I'm much too old for all this excitement. I need my shed." She gave Gubble a cold look. "Even if it does have a nasty hole in it. A troll-shaped hole."

"Excellent!" Elsie rubbed her hands together. "I'm sure someone there will look after Hinny until Marcus is better. So that's settled, and I think we're just about ready to be off." She peered around to make sure that she had sorted out everything and everyone. "Now, have I forgotten anything?"

"Yup." Marlon was flying low. "Gotta problem . . ."

Even as he spoke, a thin bony hand rose out of the crevasse where Fiddleduster Squint had fallen. It stretched up and grasped at the roots of a thornbush. A second hand clutched a twisted branch, and the zombie's head slowly emerged from the darkness.

"Feel free to depart," Fiddleduster sneered. "One has work to do here." And he looked pointedly at Trunkly, who began to tremble.

Gracie, sitting on the path beside the semiconscious Marcus, felt a cold chill sweep over her. What could she do? Even if she threw herself between Fiddleduster and the giants, how long could she hold out against him? "Think, Gracie," she told herself, "think . . ."

Fiddleduster was steadily hauling himself up hand over hand; one more minute and he would be slithering out onto the grass where the giants were sitting. The shadow was already shimmering beside them.

Gracie took a quick breath. "Meggymould! Greatover!" she shouted. "Stand up! Stand up and STAMP! Stamp as hard as you can!"

It was no use. The giants were still pondering the previous events. Fast action was not in their nature; Gracie might as well have called to the trees or the hills.

"Miss Gracie!" It was Alf. "There's a thread—a silver thread! On the path. By your hand!"

Gracie looked down and saw the delicate silver thread shining brightly. With a gasp she snatched it up and ran toward Fiddleduster as he began to pull himself out onto the solid ground. The zombie threw his head back and snarled, showing sharp yellow teeth. As Gracie thrust the shining silver as close as she dared to his burning eyes, he was forced to hold up a hand to protect himself. The root in his other hand loosened, scattering earth, and with a muffled

curse he lost his grip. Screaming a long, despairing scream, he fell down and down into the darkness.

Instinct made Gracie throw the thread after him. There was a second scream, followed by silence. A puff of purplish smoke drifted up from the depths of the hole, twisted in the sunshine, then faded away into nothingness.

"Goodness me!" It was Auntie Elsie. "If I hadn't forgotten all about that thread! Well done, Alf!"

"Alf to the rescue!" The little bat did his second victory roll of the day. "Hey! Look at Mr. Prince!"

Gracie, who had been watching in fascination as the crumbling sides of the crevasse slowly moved toward each other, shook herself and ran back.

Marcus was sitting bolt upright, looking extremely cheerful. "Hello, Gracie," he said. "Isn't it weird? I feel absolutely fine! Did we win? We did, didn't we? Hooray!"

"Are you really all right?" Gracie inspected Marcus doubtfully.

The prince jumped off the path. "As soon as that purple smoke wafted about, I felt wonderful! Well, I could do with a good night's sleep, but I bet you could too." He glanced around. "Oh! That's so odd . . . where's the hole in the ground gone?" He tucked

Gracie's arm comfortably into his, and the two of them walked together across the grass. There was no sign of the crevasse; only the thornbush marked the spot where it had been and where Fiddleduster had fallen. "WOW!" Marcus exclaimed. "We didn't dream it, did we?"

Gracie shook her head. "No."

"Ug." Gubble had come to join them. "No dream."

Marcus looked down. "Hello, Gubble. You're a hero, you know. If it hadn't been for you, we'd have—" He paused and bent to look more closely at the silver cup still firmly wedged on Gubble's green head. "Gubble, where did you find this? Can I have a look?"

"Not come off." The troll peered up with his one visible eye. "Stuck. Fell on Gubble."

Marcus did his best not to laugh. "Here, I'll pull it off for you." He took hold of the cup and gave it a sharp tug. Gubble's head came off. The cup didn't.

"OW!" said the head. "Still stuck."

"I'm so sorry," Marcus apologized. "Maybe if Gracie holds your ears, and I pull?"

This was more successful, and the cup came away with the *pop!* of a cork leaving a bottle. Gubble put his head back on with a satisfied "URF."

Marcus turned the cup around to look at the

inscription. "I thought I recognized it! It's the Five Kingdoms' Challenge Cup—it belongs to Albion's dad. Look, it says here: King Dowby! It's his pride and joy. Where did you find it, Gubble?"

Gubble shrugged. "Bad place. Howling place. Bag . . . Gubble walk over bag. Lots of shiny things fall out. Big man cross. VERY cross. Throw things at Gubble. POOR Gubble!"

Marcus let out a long whistle. "The Howling Arms! You must have found someone's stash from a robbery!"

"Yoo-hoo!" Auntie Elsie was calling. "Come along! The path's getting impatient!"

Marcus was concentrating much too hard to hear her. He turned the cup over and over, still whistling as he worked something out in his mind. "You know what," he said at last, "I reckon we should go back to Cockenzie Rood. Gubble, did you say there were lots of silver things?"

Gubble nodded.

"That's it!" Marcus's eyes were shining. "Gracie, do you think the path would take us? Or we could ride . . . Oh! Where's Hinny?"

"Auntie Vera's taking her back," Gracie said. "She left a while ago . . . You were much too sick to ride."

She pulled at the end of her braid, puzzled by the prince's excitement. "What are you planning?"

Marcus waved the cup in the air. "Don't you see? If I can find the rest of this stuff, I can take it back to King Dowby, and I'll be some kind of a hero, and Father won't be angry with me anymore. And then, maybe, he'll let me do what I want."

For a moment Gracie was so astonished that she could think of nothing to say. "But . . ." she began, "but you've already done so much! The giants! You've saved the kingdoms!"

"Father'll never believe that." There was no bitterness in Marcus's voice; he was merely stating a fact. "Honestly, Gracie." He squeezed her hand. "It's true. You know it is. Father won't ever admit there's anything strange outside the kingdoms. He never has, and he's not going to change now."

Gracie's experience of King Frank was limited, but she had seen enough to suspect that Marcus was right. "Yes," she said. "Yes. Hang on a moment——" And she ran to where Auntie Elsie was waiting. "Auntie Elsie, do you trust me?"

"Of course, my love." The Oldest smiled fondly at Gracie. "You're going to ask me to take you back to Gorebreath, aren't you?"

Gracie shook her head. "Not Gorebreath. Cockenzie Rood. Do you think we can?"

"We can try."

The path gave an encouraging wriggle, and Gracie waved to Marcus to come and join her. He settled himself beside her, and Gubble climbed on behind. Slowly the path lifted, then sank, then lifted once more before lying still.

"Are we too heavy?" Gracie asked.

"You don't weigh nothing, kiddo." Marlon fluttered down. "Ask my opinion, it's the troll."

Alf, who had appointed himself chief guardian of the path, squeaked crossly at his uncle. "It's just tired, Unc! That silver thread was from the web of power! Weighed a ton, it did! If it managed that, it can carry anything!"

Elsie was frowning. "I think it'll be all right if it can just get off the ground," she said. "But you might be right. Maybe it's worn out. Come along, Path! Try and lift up, there's a dear. Lift! LIFT?"

Greatover, who had been sitting watching what was going on with uncomprehending eyes, understood something at last. Slowly he got to his feet. Very carefully, so as not to scare the little people, he moved toward them. "LIFT."

Elsie and Gubble shut their eyes as the huge fingers took hold of the path and raised it gently into the air. Gracie and Marcus watched the ground falling away; the path felt horribly limp, and Gracie held her breath. Then there was a wriggle, a twitch, and they were flying. Not fast but very steadily . . . and Gracie relaxed.

"There we are," Elsie said. "And now I suggest we all have a little snooze. It's been a long night."

"Thank you!" Gracie shouted as loudly as she could. "THANK YOU!"

Greatover lifted an enormous hand but said nothing.

Meggymould looked at him. "BAD THING GONE!" he announced. "BAD THING ALL GONE!"

"YES." Greatover nodded, then nodded again. "IS GOOD."

Trunkly heaved herself up. "GIRL SAY EGGSIES! GO FIND EGGSIES?"

"LATER," Greatover told her. "LATER. NOW WALK."

"WALK," agreed Meggymould, and the three giants began slowly walking back to where they had come from.

Greatover was the first to sing. A vast tuneless

droning echoed over the barren landscape—tuneless, but not unpleasant. It was the sound of wind on a mountain—a wind that wandered over rocky crags and treeless summits, endlessly searching for a place to rest and to sleep.

"IS HAPPY," Trunkly said, and joined in. "WOOOO . . . WOOOO . . . WOOOOOOO . . ."

Chapter Thirty

Auntie Vera did not hurry Hinny. Their progress was slow, as befitted a tired pony and an ancient bat, and they arrived at the palace much later in the day, just as the duchess and her impromptu party were settling down for afternoon tea. The distant rumblings and trembling of the earth early that morning had upset them all; several tiles had fallen off the palace roof, and the stable chimney had collapsed. The ensuing calm had been reassuring, but Nina-Rose was still inclined to scream at the slightest sound and throw herself into Arioso's willing arms. Albion was refusing to leave his bedroom; his cousin had made a couple of attempts to persuade him out, but he had locked the door.

"What IS the matter with the boy?" Hortense asked Bluebell, exasperated.

Bluebell shook her head. "Leave him to sulk," she advised. "Whatever it is, he'll get hungry soon enough, and then he'll come out." She frowned. "I just wish we had some news about Marcus and Gracie."

There had been much discussion as to Marcus's whereabouts; his father was of the opinion that he was afraid to come home because he knew he would be in trouble. His mother was not so certain. She suspected Bluebell and the duchess knew far more than they were prepared to say, and as the day went on and Bluebell grew more and more silent, so Queen Mildred's anxiety increased.

By teatime even King Frank was beginning to have his doubts. The sight of the riderless pony trotting up the drive was more than enough to make him regret his outburst of the night before, and he almost leaped from his chair. His plate of cucumber sandwiches and chocolate cake were left uneaten as he hurried to see if there was a note or any other message suggesting where the pony had come from, but there was no clue.

Arry had followed his father; seeing Auntie Vera fluttering into the distance, her task completed, he called to her. "Bat! I say, Bat? What happened? Where's Marcus?"

Auntie Vera, offended at this form of address, took no notice and vanished into the vegetable garden.

"Arry?" King Frank looked around in surprise. "Who are you talking to?"

"Erm . . . thought I saw someone I knew," the prince said lamely.

"Someone called Bat?" the king asked, with more than a hint of sarcasm.

Arioso blinked. Maybe it was time to stand up for his brother. "Actually, Father," he said, "it might have been a friend of Marcus's. He talks to bats, you know."

The king's eyebrows rose. "Marcus talks to bats?"

"Yes," Arry said. "And so do I. Sometimes. They can be very useful. In fact, it was a bat who brought me the message about Albion needing help."

The king was beginning to feel his grip on reality loosening. "Are you telling me, in all seriousness, that a bat brought you a message from Marcus?"

Arioso nodded. "Yes."

"The boy's right, you know." Queen Bluebell was standing behind them. "Marcus has quite a few bat messengers, including a cheerful little fellow called Alf." She sighed. "Think what we've been missing all these years, Frank."

The king pulled himself together. "You can believe what you want, Bluebell old girl, but I'll believe it when I see it. Until then, as far as I'm concerned, it's a load of nonsense. Utter nonsense! I'm going to ask Hortense to send out a search party." And he marched back indoors, followed by a drooping Arioso.

Bluebell snorted and made her way around to the vegetable garden. There she peered from left to right, wondering where a bat might be found. Seeing the garden shed, complete with a Gubble-shaped hole at either end, she opened the door and looked inside. There was an irritable flutter in a dark corner; Bluebell remained politely in the doorway. "Excuse me for bothering you," she said in her mildest tones, "but I'm a friend of Prince Marcus and Gracie Gillypot. I would be most obliged if you could tell me if they are safe."

"On their way back to the House of the Ancient Crones." The squeak was so high-pitched, Bluebell had to strain to hear the words. "They did in the zombie, though. Did him in good and proper. Now, some of us need to catch up on our sleep, drafts and all. Rotten troll! Still, they couldn't have done it without him. Saved the day. Good night!"

The way in which Auntie Vera wrapped her wings around herself and turned away convinced the queen there was no point in asking any other questions. All the same, she felt wonderfully reassured and left the shed wondering how she could best convey the news to Marcus's parents.

The sound of voices in the distance made her stop to listen. One voice she recognized, or thought she did. "Marcus? How can that be? No . . . I must be wrong."

A moment later a small familiar figure zoomed over her head, circled, and then, to her intense delight, settled on her shoulder. "Hi there, Mrs. Queen," Alf squeaked. "You'll never guess what happened! Never!"

Bluebell was unable to resist. "Let me think," she said. "Aha! Could it be that Marcus and Gracie have defeated a zombie?"

Alf's squeak of astonishment made her blink. "Mrs. Queen! You're the BEST! However did you know?"

The queen chuckled. "Aha. And now they're on their way to the House of the Ancient Crones!"

"What?" Alf fluttered off her shoulder and hovered in front of her nose. "No, no, Mrs. Queen! Look! LOOK! They're here!" And he pointed with a wing to where Marcus and Gracie were struggling up the path, carrying a large and obviously heavy bag between them. Gubble stumped behind them, a look of great satisfaction on his flat green face as he hauled a bulging suitcase over the ruts and stones.

Bluebell was speechless.

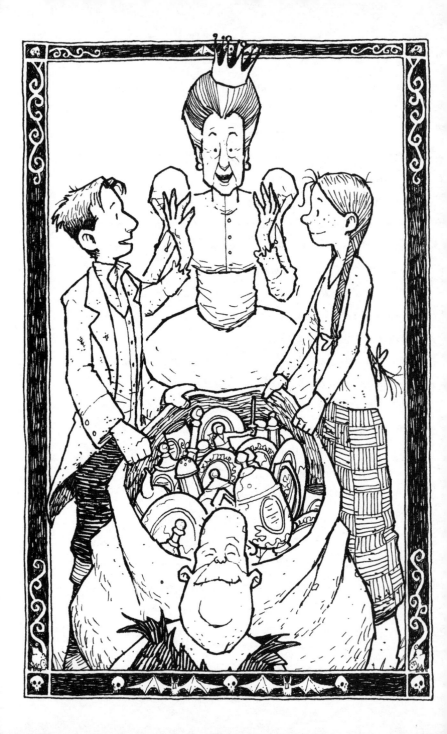

"Hello, Your Maj!" Marcus said as he and Gracie drew level with the queen. "Guess what we've found?"

The queen had a flash of inspiration. "King Dowby's trophies!" she said. "My goodness me! Were they at the Howling Arms?"

Marcus was as astonished as Alf had been. "WOW!" he said. "How did you guess?" He paused. "Well, to be honest, they were thrown around outside. Gubble made a bit of a hole in the walls, and the landlord got a bit cross and chucked everything at him, including the silver. But how did you know?"

Bluebell beamed at him. "There was a trail, and Hortense and I were following it . . . but we never got as far as the Howling Arms. Well done, Marcus! Hortense will be thrilled! Come on up to the palace. Oh! Did you know your parents are here? And Arioso?"

"They are? What's going on?" Marcus looked suddenly anxious.

"They were worried about you," Bluebell told him. "In fact, we'd better hurry. Your father's about to call out a search party. But tell me quickly, how was your adventure? Alf says it went well."

Gracie nodded. "It did, thank you. But only because of Marcus and Gubble, and Marlon and Alf. Gubble was a HERO."

Gubble grunted a bashful denial, but there was no doubt that he was pleased.

"And you, Gracie," Marcus said. "You were . . . amazing." He smiled at her, and Queen Bluebell's ancient heart warmed when she saw the way Gracie smiled back, her cheeks very pink.

"They'll be all right, those two," she said to herself. "As long as the boy's father doesn't spoil everything."

There was a determined expression on Queen Bluebell's face as she led the way back to the palace. She opened the dining-room door with a flourish and boomed, "Look who we have here! Prince Marcus, Miss Gracie Gillypot, and the very splendid Gubble!"

Queen Mildred rushed at Marcus and hugged him with tears in her eyes, and then hugged Gracie. King Frank raised an eyebrow at such an excessive demonstration of affection, but he shook Marcus's hand and slapped him on the back. The duchess winked at Bluebell and ordered more teacups to be brought.

Arry was the next to greet his brother. Nina-Rose refused to detach herself from his arm, so he brought her with him. "Very nice to see you again, bro. And you, Gubble. And you too, Gracie. Erm . . . do you know Nina-Rose?"

"I think we've met before, haven't we?" Gracie did her best to be polite, but Nina-Rose's smile was frosty.

"We might have," she said. "I don't really remember things like that." She stared pointedly at Gracie's rubber boots. "Have you been hiking?"

Gracie blushed to the roots of her hair. "Oh! Oh, I'm so sorry! I should have taken them off! That's so rude of me! I didn't mean—"

"Of course you didn't, and it doesn't matter in the least." Hortense came hurrying forward. "But would you like to change your shoes?" She took Gracie's arm and whisked her neatly away from the chilling disapproval of Nina-Rose. "Come with me, dear."

Before Gracie could think of any excuses, the duchess was showing her a wide selection of shoes and pressing her to try them on.

"Actually, my dear," the duchess said as she handed Gracie a choice of practical oxfords and a pair of furry slippers, "I'm delighted to have the chance for a private word. Please say you forgive me!"

Startled, Gracie gazed at the duchess. "Forgive you? But what for?"

"First you were turned away from my door, and then you had to sleep in a shed." Hortense shook her head. "So shocking . . ."

Gracie took the duchess's hand. "It was fine, truly. Why, if I hadn't been in the shed, I'd never have seen Albion being kidnapped!"

Hortense squeezed her hand in return. "You've been wonderful, Gracie. And I mean that most sincerely. Bluebell and I both admire you very much, indeed, and I do so hope you'll join us here on Cockenzie Rood Day for her birthday party — not that she wants one, poor thing. She can't bear the idea of all that fuss and bother. Now, I'd better get back to my guests, but please, PLEASE choose whatever you like . . . I'll be most offended if you don't!"

As the duchess swept away, Gracie studied the furry slippers. They were remarkably similar to the ones she had lost, and she was certain that Auntie Val would approve. With a small sigh she put them on. Then, aware of being watched, she looked up to find Albion standing in the doorway. "Prince Albion!" she said in surprise. "How are you feeling? Do you feel better?"

Albion frowned. Gracie Gillypot was the last person he had expected to see in his cousin's dressing room. "No. No, I don't feel at all better. I was treated very badly, you know."

For a moment Gracie said nothing. Plainly the prince was upset, but her instinct told her that it was something more than mere pique. "Yes," she agreed. "You were."

Still suspicious, Albion came a little nearer. "What was my cousin talking to you about?"

"Oh . . . shoes. And she asked me to come to Cockenzie Rood Day." Suddenly, Gracie remembered the scarlet cloaks. "It sounds very exciting. You're going to have a grand parade, aren't you?"

Albion's bravado dropped away, and he went pale. "How did you know?" he demanded. "Who told you?"

Gracie, disconcerted that she had unwittingly discovered a secret, chose her answer carefully. "My aunties are making the cloaks," she said, "but we haven't told anyone about them. Is it a surprise?"

The prince scowled. "It's not going to happen now."

"But why ever not?"

Gracie sounded genuinely concerned, and Albion shifted uneasily from one foot to the other. He had never had a sympathetic listener, especially one with compassionate blue eyes. His cousin was the epitome of brusque, and his father never spoke to him unless there was information to be passed on.

Gracie saw his hesitation. "I don't really know anything about these things," she said. "But I'd think a parade would be perfect. Are you going to lead it?" And she gave Albion one of her sweetest smiles.

Albion, dazzled, threw caution to the winds. "Can I show you something?" Gracie nodded, and he hurried out of the room. Seconds later he was back, wearing his brand-new uniform jacket and twirling his sword. "What do you think?"

"I think," Gracie said, with more tact than accuracy, "you look magnificent. And I don't think you should cancel the parade."

Albion threw his sword down in despair. "But it's all turned into a celebration of Queen Bluebell's birthday! It's not about Cockenzie Rood at all! They want the band to play 'Happy Birthday'!"

Gracie picked up the sword and handed it back to him. "That doesn't sound to me like much of a celebration for Cockenzie Rood Day. The crowd'll want to cheer and shout and whistle and feel that they're the MOST important of the Five Kingdoms. So why don't you have your parade, and at the very end you can salute the crowd—and then, if she doesn't mind, you could salute Queen Bluebell. Your cousin told me the queen doesn't want any fuss—she'd absolutely hate it if the band played 'Happy Birthday.'"

There was a very long pause. Gracie wondered if she'd said too much or said it all wrong . . . but then Albion stood up straight. "Do you know what, Gracie

Gillypot? You're a very clever girl. That's EXACTLY what I was thinking."

Gracie suppressed a smile. "I'm so glad."

"And I'm going to tell Cousin Hortense right now this minute," Albion went on. He tucked the sword under his arm and headed for the door, only to stop with his hand on the handle. "Erm . . . would you mind coming with me? It's very odd, but you make me feel better."

"Of course I'll come with you," Gracie said, and the two of them marched side by side to the dining room.

Albion's announcement was greeted by both Hortense and Bluebell with the most satisfactory enthusiasm. Even the twenty scarlet cloaks were accepted as entirely appropriate and very suitable for the occasion. Queen Mildred and King Frank also applauded the idea of a grand parade and made a mental note to have one themselves the following year.

Only Princess Nina-Rose looked disapproving. "But I want the band to play 'Happy Birthday to You,'" she said. "After all, it was my idea!" She tugged at Arioso's arm. "YOU thought it was a BRILLIANT idea, didn't you, Arry darling?"

Bluebell got up from the chair she had been sitting

in. "Rubbish!" she boomed. "I'd say Albion's idea is first class. It's Cockenzie Rood Day, not Bluebell day!"

"Well done, Albion," King Frank agreed. "A prince who thinks of his kingdom! Excellent. Excellent!"

Albion glowed. He puffed out his chest and basked in the unaccustomed approval. "It's going to be the best Cockenzie Rood Day ever," he declared. "Ahem. I look forward to welcoming you all to the grandest parade in the Five Kingdoms. Even you, Marcus. Oh, and Gracie, of course." He waved a gracious hand. "Yes. You must be sure to come. You're a good girl, Gracie. A very good girl."

"What's she got to do with anything?" Nina-Rose asked in a piercing whisper. "I do wish someone would tell me why she's here. And that green thing. It gives me the creeps."

"Gubble," Queen Bluebell said loudly, "is a very remarkable troll. Gubble dear, would you mind fetching the bag and the suitcase that we left outside the door?"

Gubble grunted and did as he was told. Bluebell opened the bag, pulled out a silver cup, and handed it to the duchess. "Here you are, Hortense, old gal."

Hortense gasped. "Bluebell! It's Dowby's Challenge Cup! You've found it!"

"No." Bluebell raised her voice to full volume, and

the room was silenced. "Marcus found it. In fact, he found all the stolen silver. You should be very proud of your son, Frank!" She tipped the contents of the bag and the suitcase onto the carpet. Flagons, cups, bowls, teapots, medals, jugs, and soup tureens tumbled out in a gleaming heap of bejeweled silver. "There you are! All safe and sound."

"Goodness me!" Hortense looked at it in wonder. "I'd no idea he'd taken so many things! Thank you, Marcus, my dear. I'm very, VERY grateful."

This was something that King Frank could understand and appreciate. He coughed and held out his hand to Marcus for the second time that day. "Well done, lad. Didn't realize you were after a thief. Splendid stuff, splendid! Erm . . . yes. Let's forget about everything I said before. Feel free to come and go. Yes. Good work, indeed."

Marcus shook his father's hand warmly. "Thanks, Father." He looked across at Bluebell and smiled at her. "And thank you too, ma'am."

Bluebell beamed and gave him a conspiratorial wink.

Marcus grinned and took Gracie's hand in his. "And now, if it's OK with everyone, I'd like to take Gracie home . . . Someone's waiting for her." He did not add that he was expecting to travel on a flying path, accompanied by two bats and an Ancient Crone.

This was not at all what King Frank had expected, but he was still feeling magnanimous. "Of course, dear boy! Off you go. And good-bye, Gracie. Thanks to you too, of course."

Albion was not entirely sorry to see Marcus taking his leave of the assembled company. The discovery of the missing silver had removed him from his place in the sun, and he was hoping to retrieve it. He was, however, genuinely sad to see Gracie go. He rushed after her and Marcus, and hovered in the doorway. "So you'll definitely come to see my parade?" he asked anxiously. "You will come, Gracie?"

"Of course I will," Gracie promised.

"We'll both come," Marcus told him.

Albion dithered. "Yes. Good. So I'll see you soon . . . Well, good-bye!"

Queen Bluebell, seeing that Albion was showing no signs of removing himself, stalked over and imposed her substantial bulk in front of him. "Don't let us keep you, my dears," she said firmly. "Good luck . . . and come and see me soon. Don't forget, now!"

Gracie stood on her tiptoes and kissed the queen. "Thank you. We will!" She gave a sudden giggle. "We'll send Alf to say we're coming!"

"I'd enjoy that." Bluebell nodded. "I'd enjoy that very much, indeed."

As Gubble shut the door and followed them down the steps, Marcus heaved a huge sigh of relief. "Wow! Thank goodness that's over. Oh! It is OK if I come back with you, isn't it?"

"Of course it is," Gracie told him. "The aunties will be ever so pleased to see you."

Marcus held her hand a little tighter. "I wasn't really worrying about them. I was wondering about you, Gracie. I—I really need to know. YOU'LL be pleased, won't you?"

Gracie looked at him, her eyes very clear and blue. "Oh, yes," she said. "I'll be pleased. In fact, I'll be very pleased, indeed."

"Good," Marcus said. And then, "You kissed Queen Bluebell."

"I know," Gracie said. "I'm very fond of her."

Marcus said nothing.

Gracie blushed, then began to laugh. "OK," she said. "OK . . ." And she kissed him too.

High above their heads, Alf flew the biggest victory roll of his entire life. "YES!" he squeaked. "YES!"

Chapter Thirty-one

The Ancient One was sitting with her feet up reading the *Cockenzie Rood Daily Register*. "'The Royal Parade was, without a doubt, the outstanding event of Cockenzie Rood Day,'" she reported to Elsie, who was curling her wig on the other side of the kitchen table. "'Prince Albion is a true prince and will one day be worthy to take his place as king.' Oho! Listen to this, Elsie! 'Twenty chosen members of the guard wore scarlet cloaks, and a fine sight they were as they marched up and down while our noble prince took the salute in the absence of his father, King Dowby. Tribute was paid to Queen Bluebell, one of the guests, on the occasion of her eighty-first birthday; a cake was presented during the evening's entertainments. Among the many guests were—' Are you listening, Elsie?"

"Of course I am," Elsie said.

The Ancient One put the newspaper down and inspected her companion. "You're spending a lot of time on that wig. May I ask why?"

Elsie twirled a curl around her finger. "You never know," she said as casually as she could. "I might want to go out somewhere again. I rather enjoyed my little adventure, but I'd have looked less of a fright if I'd had my wig."

"It would have blown away while you were flying on the path," Edna said in crushing tones. "If you're going to have adventures, you'd be better off without it."

Elsie brightened. "So you wouldn't mind if I popped out from time to time? Not too often, of course . . ."

"Of course." The Ancient One went back to her paper. "Now, listen to this . . . 'Among the many guests was Prince Arioso, heir to the kingdom of Gorebreath. On his arm was his fiancée, Princess Nina-Rose of Dreghorn. Also present was Prince Marcus, escorting Miss Gracie Gillypot. Will we be hearing double wedding bells in the not-too-distant future?'" Edna flung the paper down. "Really!"

Elsie put on her wig and peered at her reflection in a saucepan before taking it off again. "But don't you think she might marry Marcus one day?"

"She might, or then again she might not," Edna said, "but she's got far more sense than to have a double wedding with those two sticks of celery."

Elsie laughed and picked up the rejected newspaper. "I'm sure you're right. What other news is there? Oh, well I never! 'The Howling Arms is open once more after general refurbishment.' That means they've blocked up the holes Gubble made in the walls."

"That reminds me," Edna said, looking at the damaged kitchen door. "We really must get that mended."

Elsie wasn't listening. "'Gruntle Marrowgrease Welcomes You All! His new staff member, Aloysius Bullstrop, will be delighted to take your orders, while Marley Bagsmith will provide every support in the kitchen.' You'd need to hang on to your handbag if you went anywhere near that lot."

"And you'd need to hang on to your wig," the Ancient One retorted with a chuckle. "I'm going to check the web." She heaved herself out of her chair and stomped off to room seventeen. Val was working at the web of power, and Foyce was sulking in front of a piece of purple cloth.

"All well?" Edna asked cheerfully.

Val nodded. "Smooth as a summer's day," she said. "Isn't it beautiful?"

It was true. The silver rippled and shone, every so often throwing out a sparkle like a tiny star.

"It looks positively happy," Edna said thoughtfully. "Maybe good things are on the way."

Val stuck out her slipper-clad feet. "I did get my slippers back," she said, "and they're better than ever, so that's a good thing. Gracie must have taken great care of them."

"I don't think that was quite what I had in mind," the Ancient One said, "but I'm delighted. How are you getting on, Foyce?"

"Can't see why that stupid Prince Albion wants a purple cloak," Foyce complained. "He'll look hideous."

Edna ignored her remarks and bent to look at the weaving. "Well done," she said in surprise. "You're coming on well! This is splendid!"

Foyce was, for once, speechless.

"There!" Val looked pleased with herself. "That's another good thing!"

"Hmm," said the Ancient One. "I still think there might be something else . . ."

Sitting under a tall tree, Marcus and Gracie were throwing pinecones into a stream. Gubble sat beside them, while Marlon and Alf argued aimiably above their heads.

"What shall we do tomorrow?" Marcus asked idly.

Gracie giggled. "Anything you like, just as long as I don't have to watch Albion marching up and down and up and down and—"

"Up and down and up and down," Marcus finished her sentence. "I know."

"Still, he did enjoy it," Gracie said. "Maybe his father will take some notice of him now."

Marcus made a face. "Dowby? He'll probably want mounted cavalry next year and make poor old Albion miserable again. Do you think he'll ever find out that all his trophies went missing?"

"I think the duchess or Queen Bluebell will tell him." Gracie gave the prince a sideways glance. "They want to make sure everyone remembers it was you who found them." She did not add, "Especially your father," but the words hung in the air.

"Gubble found them, really." Marcus threw a pine-cone right across the stream. "He's much more of a hero than I am."

Gubble turned purple. "Not hero. Am Gubble."

"So you are," Gracie told him.

Marcus picked up another cone, and began pulling off pieces. "I did wonder," he said slowly, "if you'd like to ride out and visit the giants. See how they're getting on."

Gracie's eyes lit up. "Oh, YES!" she said. "That's a brilliant idea!"

"Really?" Marcus dropped his pinecone and jumped to his feet. "Then, that's what we'll do!"

He suddenly started to laugh, and Gracie looked at him in surprise. "What's up?"

"Can you imagine," Marcus said, in between paroxysms of laughter, "what Nina-Rose would say if Arry asked her to go and see some giants? Oh, Gracie Gillypot, I'm so glad you're the way you are. You're the very, very, VERY best, and do you know what?"

Gracie shook her head. Up on the branch above, Marlon and Alf froze. Gubble gazed upward, his small piggy eyes as wide as they would go.

"I love you," Marcus said. "I really, really do. Come on. Let's go!"

And he and Gracie walked away between the trees . . .